THE ISLANDS OF

Divine Music

John Addiego

THE ISLANDS OF

Divine Music

JOHN ADDIEGO

UNBRIDLED
BOOKS

This is a work of fiction. The names, characters, places and incidents are either the product of the author's imagination or are used fictitiously, and any resemblance to actual persons living or dead, business establishments, events, or locales is entirely coincidental.

Unbridled Books
Denver, Colorado

Copyright © 2008 John Addiego

Library of Congress Cataloging-in-Publication Data
Addiego, John.
The islands of divine music by / John Addiego.
p.   cm.
ISBN 978-1-932961-54-6
1. Italians—United States—Fiction.   2. Italian Americans—Fiction.
3. Italian American families—Fiction.   4. Family—Fiction.   I. Title.
PS3601.D46I85   2008
813'.6—dc22
2008018617

1   3   5   7   9   10   8   6   4   2

Book Design by SH • CV

First Printing

The Family is the Country of the heart.

GIUSEPPE MAZZINI

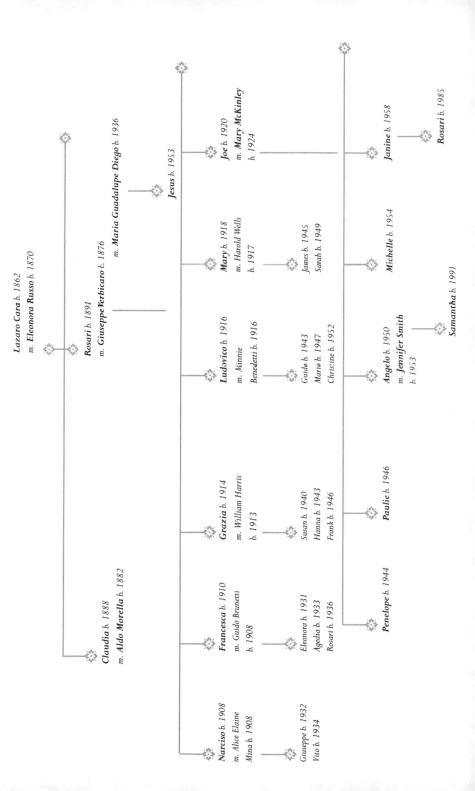

Lazaro Cara b. 1862
m. Eleonora Russo b. 1870

Claudia b. 1888
m. Aldo Morella b. 1882

Rosari b. 1891
m. Giuseppe Verbicaro b. 1876
m. Maria Guadalupe Diego b. 1936

Jesus b. 1953

Narciso b. 1908
m. Alice Elaine
Mina b. 1908

Giuseppe b. 1932
Vito b. 1934

Francesca b. 1910
m. Guido Brunetti
b. 1908

Eleonora b. 1931
Agedia b. 1933
Rosari b. 1936

Grazia b. 1914
m. William Harris
b. 1913

Susan b. 1940
Hanna b. 1943
Frank b. 1946

Ludovico b. 1916
m. Minnie
Benedetti b. 1916

Guido b. 1943
Marie b. 1947
Christine b. 1952

Mary b. 1918
m. Harold Wells
b. 1917

James b. 1945
Sarah b. 1949

Joe b. 1920
m. Mary McKinley
b. 1924

Penelope b. 1944

Paulie b. 1946

Angelo b. 1950
m. Jennifer Smith
b. 1953

Samantha b. 1991

Michelle b. 1954

Janine b. 1958

Rosari b. 1985

THE ISLANDS OF
Divine Music

A ROSE IN THE NEW WORLD

Rosari

S ome came from the bottom of the boot to find a new life when theirs was unbearable, and some whispered the word *America* over and over among their prayers and sought to present themselves new before God in a new world. Rosari left Southern Italy and set sail into the unknown for an additional reason: in order to escape prosecution for her prodigality.

Her father, Lazaro Cara, was a gentle man, and some would say he was too gentle. When his wife left him he gave up the chase after a week of weeping and lugging his children from village to village in the hilly south of Italy. Rosari's mother was a beautiful woman with wildly sad eyes, with thick black curls which played across her cheeks even when she tried to keep them bound in a scarf. She dropped the wash in Rosari's arms one day, put on her nicest dress, and left. Friends and family lent her father a jackass and a shotgun, but he looked silly holding the firearm in his arms like a baby wrapped in bunting. He wept, and Rosari and her older sister wept, and they walked from town to town with the jackass and ate cold potatoes and handouts from strangers and milk from their nanny goat, then returned home.

Lazaro returned to his vocation, which was cutting the hair of the merchants and land barons and gossips in Reggio Calabria. Word came that his wife had run off with a man named Gulia. Then word was she'd dumped Gulia, or there had never been a Gulia, or that a fat butcher named Benedetti in Napoli, who already had a wife and seven children, was keeping her as a mistress, or that she had been seen among gypsies singing at a saint's-day fair near Eboli. Then a cholera epidemic hit, and the stories about his wife got swept out the doorway with the hair and were replaced by stories of death.

The disease took the life of Rosari's cousin Paolo and a new-born neighbor named Gino Emilio Ravetto. Lazaro had little work and less money, the village had more activity in the cemetery with its ornate crypts and sepulchres than it did in its piazza, so, two years after his wife had left them, he and Rosari and Claudia rode a freight train to Napoli, a crowded, filthy, dangerous place. Maybe they were going to beg her mother to come back from the butcher, Rosari thought, maybe they were looking for people who still cared about the condition of their hair, or maybe they were simply taking their grief to the open road as they had when her mother had left. They hopped onto the moving train and the father held his two girls and wept for miles along the steep and sooty coastline.

Every dark eye and flowing tress in the city made Rosari's heart jump for want of her mother. Around the corner would come a young woman holding a basket filled with mushrooms or Swiss chard, and for a moment the girl would think it was she. Through the window of the barbershop where her father snipped hair and she cleaned the floor and shined shoes she might see a woman's profile, somebody in a black dress with a load of firewood balanced on her head, and Rosari would almost cry out, *Mama!* Most of the time she kept her feelings to herself, and mostly because she didn't want her father to get started and have him cry all over the head of some rich customer, but the keening for her mother overtook her now and then in the crowded apartment above the barbershop, and the fact that Claudia soon left them didn't help.

Her sixteen-year-old sister was engaged to a Neapolitan stonemason within a month of their arrival. Plump, quiet, simpleminded Claudia got married and moved into her mother-in-law's house the night of the wedding. Rosari, who had learned to read by age seven with the help of her father and the sisters at Santo Giovanni, her home church, lost herself in newspapers and books as a way to cope with the loss of her sister and the lost hope of finding their mother. She found many books to choose among in the big city, on racks in a tobacconist's, in the houses of the merchants. The girl would run down the narrow streets, dodging carts and mules, and deliver clean linen to ladies who would lend her books about knights and damsels in distress. She was just eleven years old, a dark-skinned, scrawny girl with disheveled hair and her nose in a book, when Gratiano, a local criminal who liked a close shave and a shoe shine, studied her.

Debonair, articulate, yet hopelessly illiterate, Gratiano sat in the chair under Lazaro's nimble fingers and watched the girl read a

THE ISLANDS OF DIVINE MUSIC

book half as big as she was. She reads and writes? he asked the barber. At that time only one of every ten Neapolitans could read.

Smart as a whip, Lazaro replied.

If I could do that I'd learn English and go to America. And the girl thought of how she would marry this handsome man with the dark eyes and sail to America, where he would earn an honest living trading prosciutto or pelts with Indians, and she would read books in Italian and English to him and their three children.

The next morning, as she was carrying *pane rustico* from the baker's, the criminal and his friend stopped her. They were seated on the sidewalk before a bar, each man holding a demitasse. Gratiano waved her over and introduced her to the large, bald man in a blue suit. My friend doesn't believe you can write. Would you be so kind as to demonstrate? He handed her a fountain pen, such as she'd never seen before, and she wrote the words he dictated to her on a piece of butcher paper which enveloped a pig's leg. Both men clapped their hands and slapped their knees enthusiastically. Gratiano placed three lire on the table and said he'd like to pay her to write a letter for him, provided she could keep it secret. Rosari set down her loaves and straightaway put the criminal's words to pen on a piece of parchment:

Esteemed Sir, it began, *Please excuse this intrusion into your private affairs. Financial difficulties, as well as recent illnesses in my family, have forced me into the position in which I find myself. My associate and I must come to your hotel this afternoon and kidnap you. Be entirely assured that no harm will come to you, and that your freedom will be immediately reinstated once a ransom of five thousand lire, or the equivalent in your British pounds, has been transferred to you by wire from your most highly esteemed family in Great Britain. It is my greatest hope that, once I have received this money, you will continue your travels in the sunny South. Perhaps you will see the ruins at Pompeii? Of course, that is your affair, not mine. I only wish you the least inconvenience during this kidnap, as well as many happy returns to our beautiful city.*

With Sincere Regrets and Fondest Hopes,
Mr. Z

She read it back to the criminals, and they leaned back in their chairs and closed their eyes, Gratiano sighing now and then while the bald man nodded and murmured words of praise. She didn't understand some of the words she'd written, and she wondered how an Englishman might decipher their idiom, but the robust approval of the two men made her chest puff out in its baggy, hand-me-down dress. What a prodigy! Gratiano exclaimed. A genius, the bald man said, and he added two more lire to the three. But he didn't like the Mr. Z part and wanted it changed to The Shadow. Gratiano said Mr. Z was fine since nobody's name began with a Z, and he pinched the girl's cheek and winked at her. Rosari's face colored. She took her bread and money and ran back to her father, resolved to tell him nothing of the adventure.

There was constant talk of America in her neighborhood, particularly in the barbershop and the piazza. Cholera and malaria, starvation and poverty, all manner of suffering were driving rural people to the crowded city or to caves in the mountains, and as they huddled before their fires they dreamed of America. The hill folk had used the ancient cave dwellings as goat stables for as long as anyone could remember, but now the goats were being eaten or turned out for miserable human families to reclaim. Rosari had seen them from the train, the little archways dug into pale limestone cliffs high above the coastline, the women in black shawls and head coverings squatting before them. In America there would be fresh air to prevent disease, work for good money, and open space to plant gardens and keep animals, people said. Lazaro, contrary to his neighbors, maintained that he was more apt to return to his hometown than to leave the country. Once the plague has passed, and all the rats have left the sinking ship, he told his daughter, we can return to our home. Perhaps your mother will come back to us, too, he added with a sniffle.

About three weeks after she'd written Gratiano's letter a policeman came to the barbershop, and Rosari heard that an Englishman had been kidnapped from the local hotel. She swept the floor and averted her eyes. Her father told her to go upstairs and make the soup, but she wanted to hear the conversation, so she knocked over the glass filled with combs and spent another five minutes cleaning up after herself. She heard the men laugh, whistle, and cluck their tongues, but she didn't catch much of what they said.

In the books beautiful women were sometimes kidnapped by scoundrels and rescued by knights or gentlemen. Gratiano was far from a scoundrel in her eyes, and some Englishman at the hotel was hardly a beautiful woman, so she hadn't really sensed that her use of the word in the letter could amount to something like real kidnapping until now. It had seemed more likely that the word might have other meanings when used in other contexts. She prepared the soup with the wife of Fratelli the barber and brought it and the bread out to the steps where the three families usually ate in the heat of the day. There were twelve altogether, the wives and children of the two other barbers spread out along the shade of the busy street, and they all spoke of the kidnapping now, the three barbers, sworn to secrecy moments before by the carabinieri, having spilled the beans to their wives and children instantly.

Among the more urbane of the criminal society, particularly *la mano nera* of Napoli, a prekidnapping note such as Rosari had written was common practice. The wealthy victim was given a chance to put his things in order, prepare his family and finances for the inevitable, perhaps even pack a few necessities. Resistance was, essentially, futile. Organized criminals of the South could afford to extend this courtesy with little risk, and the families of victims generally paid the ransom, which was never exorbitant, immediately. But this Englishman's father hadn't followed custom; rather, he'd sent twice the ransom to local military and police, who had arrested Gratiano and his partner in the bar where they and the Englishman had been sharing a chianti and playing pinochle. The word on the street was that they would soon hang from a tree in the piazza, but that the judge was waiting to arrest a third conspirator first because, clearly, neither of these men could write their names, let alone the kidnap note found on the victim.

Rosari felt sick and asked to be excused.

For three days she didn't eat, and Lazaro sent for one of the local fortune-tellers to diagnose her illness. The old woman poured olive oil into a bowl of water and gasped at the shape it took on the surface. Lazaro, Claudia, Fratelli the barber's wife, and two of her children gasped and cried out as well, although none of them knew what the shape signified. Herbs, entrails, and other measures were recommended, but before Lazaro went to get a few coins for remedies the girl pulled him close and, weeping bitterly, confessed.

The room fell silent. Then the fortune-teller shrugged and said, Well, that would do it.

Lazaro applied for work permits to America and Argentina that very day. He would work in a steel foundry, a coal mine, a gaucho ranch, a fort surrounded by Indian tepees, anywhere, yes. And he could read and write, and he was a highly skilled barber trained by the army outside Roma when he was a youth, and he had no physical ailments, and no, he had no . . . He paused, then reported that he had no wife, that the woman had died two years previous, but that he did have one child still living with him, just a little girl. Only a simple little girl who tried to help out around the barbershop, but, bless her heart, she was very slow and stupid, poor thing.

For the next few weeks Lazaro forbade his daughter to hold a book or a newspaper. When she delivered the linen she had to turn down the romances offered by the merchants' wives, and sometimes she told the ladies that she couldn't read and had only been looking at the drawings. Articles about the kidnapping and the trial lay curled on the barbers' chairs, tempting her like the serpent in the garden, and opinions about the case were aired by the magistrates of the piazza and the orators of the street corners while their hair sloughed off their heads and fell onto the floor, but Rosari kept her mouth shut. Some said that the Englishman wanted to drop the charges and had found the experience a lark rather than an ordeal, but that his father and the police saw the matter differently. Others claimed that the police, emboldened by the infusion of money and the rhetoric of a British prefect from Rome, had suddenly remembered that Gratiano and Umberto were already under suspicion for previous crimes, particularly for perforating the bodies of a dishonest landlord and a known child molester with butchers' knives and dumping the same into the Tyrrhenian Sea.

The day before their departure two remarkable things happened, the first of which came in the form of a court summons. Father and daughter had just packed what they could into a trunk and two sheets made into shoulder sacks when a scrawny officer told them to follow him. They walked on stiff and trembling legs behind the little man's quick strides, a train of the other barbers' children, some nosy neighbors, and a few unemployed curiosity-seekers hitching behind. The little man ordered the others to stop at the foot of the steps, then led Rosari and Lazaro into the courthouse.

They descended a dank, smelly stairwell to the row of jail cells. The top of Umberto's bald head could be seen at the end of a blanket where the big man slept with his face covered. A stink of piss and excrement came from one end of the dark corridor, and Rosari pulled her scarf across her nose. The little officer had them raise their arms and, begging their pardon first, he patted their clothes, then led them to Gratiano.

The criminal sat in sleeveless shirt and suspenders, an unlit, hand-rolled cigarette between his lips. He put on his coat and fedora after he looked up and saw the visitors. Even in the squalid jail cell, with his rumpled clothes and the bruised and swollen skin about his eye and nose where the interrogators had left the mark of their work, he looked, to Rosari, the most handsome man in the world.

I wanted to thank you for your kindnesses to me. They are letting me say all the farewells I wish, he said in a husky voice. His eyes darted to the policeman, who stood a few yards off, then turned to Rosari's. He continued in a whisper, You should never worry about nothing, and he made a gesture indicating that his lips were sealed. Then, in a louder voice, he told Lazaro to be thankful for having such a little jewel of a daughter, and he tapped his forehead with his index finger. What I would give for such a mind.

God bless you, Gratiano, Lazaro exclaimed through his tears. He made the sign of the cross and kissed the criminal's hand. Tomorrow I take this little jewel with me to America.

Ah! Gratiano's eyes filled with tears. America!

They were crying when they stepped into the brilliant light and noise of Naples, and drying their eyes when they got back to the barbershop, where the second remarkable thing happened. A scrawny, hunched woman sat on the steps beside Fratelli the barber's wife. The woman's black dress and head covering hung about her bones, and though her drawn face was vaguely familiar, her eyes were the most foreign things Rosari had ever seen. These eyes had lost most of their hue, as if some brush with the sun had singed them. Nevertheless, Lazaro knelt beside the woman and repeated the word *Eleonora, Eleonora.* This was the name of Rosari's mother.

She seemed a kind of zombie. Her gestures were stiff and slow, her eyes more in the world of the dead than that of the living, and Rosari was scared of her. There was some debate that evening about whether she should stay in Naples with Claudia, whose mother-in-law clearly didn't want her, or come with her husband and youngest girl to America. The mother, sitting stiff as a mannequin on Lazaro's bed, said very little during the debate. Fratelli, who threw his weight around the shop and apartment, said in a loud voice that if he were Lazaro, he'd throw the woman back out on the street, and Lazaro stood with arms folded and said that he was considering doing just exactly that. He assumed an uncharacteristic air of severity, standing with arms crossed and chin thrust out. At one point he paced with hands behind his back, a soldier wearing a barber's apron as his uniform, and turned suddenly to point his scissors at his wife. I have not yet decided, he told her, what we shall do with you.

In the morning they started for the wharf. No decision had been made, except that Lazaro allowed Eleonora to carry one of the bundled sheets. She trailed behind her husband and daughter, bent under the burden. When they reached the gate, Lazaro produced papers, and the agent snorted at him.

It says here your wife is dead.

A mistake, Lazaro said. Look, I have our marriage certificate, and that's her. You don't believe me, ask her. Ask our daughter.

The agent stared at Eleonora. She looks wrong, he said. She looks touched in the head. They might not let her into New York.

Rosari suddenly cried and clung to her mother's arm while the woman stood stiff as a statue. The line pressed them from behind as people leaned close to witness the drama.

I don't know if she's touched in the head. I'm a barber, Lazaro said, I'm not a doctor. Are you a doctor?

The agent lifted his head toward the ceiling and asked no one in particular why he had to deal with lunatics.

Look, she disappears and comes back two years later like this. What am I supposed to do?

The agent shrugged and shook his head. Then he stamped their papers and sent them aboard.

They sat in the perpetual racket and stink of the ship's engine and the closeness of too many bodies. When allowed, Rosari went on deck with Lazaro while the mother remained seated on their belongings in the steerage hold, her knees drawn up and her face resting on her arms. It was late fall, and the Mediterranean sky glimmered like the gold-leaf dome of some Byzantine temple, but after they passed Gibraltar into the ocean a seasonal change took hold. Sky and sea turned coal gray, and North Atlantic winds stabbed them with invisible blades of ice.

Against reason, the mother now stood on deck and stared into the green-and-black face of the deep until husband and daughter found her and led her back to the hold. Sometimes she took off her head scarf and revealed the thick curls of what had once been waist-length hair now chopped to her earlobes. For a moment she might weep and let her family hold her, but more often she sat cold as marble or pushed their arms off her body. She might say a word or two about America, but mostly she'd stare off in silence with eyes that reminded Rosari of those on the sun-faded frescoes painted many generations ago on the walls of Santo Giovanni back home.

Somewhere beyond the British Isles, after days of sky dark as the sea, the ocean began to push the boat like a child on a swing. Water splashed against the high portals. The several hundred strangers sat upright like children awakened from a nightmare, barely daring to move or speak, as the ship swung from side to side. The vessel's joints creaked, and the engine wheezed like an asthmatic. Moans and prayers started to mingle with the ship's complaints, and for hours Rosari clung to her father and tried to engage her mother's cold arms as well, but Eleonora sat like a stone, and in the brief flashes of lightning her face appeared rapt, as if absorbing a beautiful music from afar.

At dawn Rosari awoke to her mother's gentle voice. She sat up and let Eleonora lead her through the softly swaying floor of bodies to the dark and icy stairway. Her mother spoke to her as she had years ago, in a sweet and animated voice. She spoke of their great adventure, their journey to a new world, and when she thrust open the door to the deck it seemed that Rosari was either deep within a dream or that she and her mother had indeed just crossed into some other world.

Eleonora stood on deck with her head uncovered, her face radiant, and the sky fell as white jewels onto her black hair. She lifted Rosari's hand, and they danced slowly through the snow, a substance Rosari had never seen before, a phenomenon which seemed to her then the flight of a million angels come to guide her mother and herself to a new life. And as the snow fell a celestial music, as of glass rubbing on silk, came down from the sky and lifted her heart.

For the remaining days of their voyage Eleonora spoke and moved with great animation. Lazaro stared at her in astonishment. The woman tended sick children and seemed equipped with special insight regarding all manner of ailments, prescribing various foods and administering healing treatments with her hands. Her beauty shone among the frightened and weary passengers like a fountain of snow in a black and leafless forest, but her eyes remained faded, as if buffeted by some otherworldly light, and her words made little sense in conversation. Often as she spoke father and daughter exchanged looks, and more than once fellow passengers touched their foreheads and nodded to each other.

The ship chugged through a fog that occasionally conjured a few gulls or even the voices of seals, and then one day the engine's racket stopped and the passengers gathered on the deck. America, they whispered to each other, was just over there, and they stood on deck a long time waiting for America to appear, the families clutching bundles, pressed together for warmth. After several hours a small launch appeared, and then others. The people were loaded onto them and carried into the fog.

Rosari's first view of America was nothing like the savage wilderness filled with Indians or the modern skyline of New York in her imagination. What she saw through the gauzy fog looked like a Russian castle trimmed with an icing of snow. The striped towers of Ellis Island made her think that they might soon be riding huge sleighs pulled by reindeer across America. Her father would cut the hair of a Russian prince while she and her mother helped the czarina choose which satin dress and which broach to wear, and Gratiano would escape from his jail and join them in America, where they would all dance in the snow with the Russian royalty.

They squeezed through a narrow entryway and climbed to a cavernous room where they were herded by beefy, pink-faced men into something like a gigantic pen for goats. Rosari could see that the room was filled with pens in which people of various look and language were placed with their fellows, people with small, flat noses, with furry caps, with eyeglasses and skullcaps. Most all of them, like her family, were wrapped in black clothing and weariness while their eyes searched the high windows for the source of the little bars of light.

Lazaro tried to coach his wife on ways to look and act, but the woman couldn't sit still for a minute. She'd pace, her mouth moving as in speech, her hands gesturing to nobody, then sit again beside her daughter. A pale-skinned man with white-blond hair opened the gate to the pen and waved his arm, and the Italians grabbed their things and followed him, but as they walked a few of them were stopped by another man in a blue suit who examined their eyes with some sort of hook. Rosari was scared to death he'd look at her mother's eyes and know she was touched, so she pulled on Eleonora's hand and yanked her into the thick of the mob.

They stood in line after line. They were asked by men in suits to open their mouths, cough, run up a stairway, as they moved along. A few weak-legged people were led to another room, and Rosari supposed they were going to be shipped back as unfit for America. When Eleonora and Rosari were examined the mother laughed gaily, and the child heaved a sigh of praise to Santa Maria. Through gates, in more lines, with Lazaro before them producing papers, they proceeded, until they sat in a smaller room filled with people speaking a dozen languages with boisterous, triumphant inflections. At the end of one long day they left the castle of Ellis Island and floated across a greasy channel of water to New York.

They had been warned by the translator on the island, but Rosari knew that her softhearted father would be no match for any vultures waiting for them on the dock. The carrion-eaters slid out of the crowd and attached themselves to the immigrants, shouting personal questions at Lazaro in a strange sort of gobbledygook Italian dialect, seeming tremendously interested in her father's background. A barber! What a beautiful occupation, but there is no money for it here, I must tell you in all honesty. Nearly as dirty as Naples, New York had the added feature of a freezing wind which sailed up Rosari's dress and made her dance under her burden as she followed her parents and the one particular shyster who'd seemed to lay claim to her family and discouraged a couple of others with his elbows. A barber! The man was huge and smelled of cigars and perfume and sweat. A barber in America gets paid nothing, even though his fingers are fast. I have a suggestion for you, Lorenzo.

Lazaro, her mother corrected the man. She seemed to be hanging on the man's words.

If I told you I know how you could make more money in one month than you made in all of last year just by using your fast fingers for something different from cutting hair, what would you say?

Both her parents chirped excitedly like small children. The man's strangled Italian seemed to Rosari a language of the new world, a tougher and more chaotic way of speaking to match the rough-and-tumble of America. In a matter of a few minutes this giant of a man, whose tongue made a kind of mechanical racket in the way it chopped Italian words and whose suit smelled a bit like the prostitutes in Naples, had arranged for jobs and an apartment for her parents, if they would only follow him. He tried to carry her mother's burden, but she wouldn't let him, so he grabbed Rosari's. A horseless coach roared past, the first motorized carriage the family had ever seen, and as they gasped and exclaimed the man laughed. He laughed like a drunk and leaned close to her father, who smiled broadly. You won't regret this, Lafcadio.

Lazaro, Eleonora said again. They pushed through the crowd.

Suddenly a woman yelled at them, a young woman who spoke their idiom as if she'd just stepped beside Eleonora to wash clothes in Reggio Calabria. Beside her was a stout Italian priest, and what the two of them said about the giant with the cigars made the serpent in the garden sound like an altar boy in comparison, but by the time Rosari had heard their accusations the giant had disappeared into the mob on the waterfront, and so had the bundle of possessions she'd been carrying.

The priest and the young woman led them to a filthy neighborhood full of desperate Irish, Poles, and Italians, some of them their fellow voyagers. Rosari thought of the women before the caves in Southern Italy as she stared at these women taking down frozen wash, trousers stiff as planks, between the brown walls of an alley. In the church there was a floor to sleep on, and as the new world was turning their fingers blue, and as they'd just lost one-third of everything they owned, they accepted the church's generosity with many thanks.

It was as if they'd returned to the ship, crowded as they were on the floor with the other immigrant families, and Rosari could feel the rocking motion of the ocean as she lay down. She heard the hissed tones of strange tongues as she drifted in and out of sleep. Her mother paced among the pews and peered out the windows of the door. At times she returned to her husband and child, and Rosari could hear her chastise Lazaro for not accepting the great opportunity offered them by the giant on the waterfront. Before her weary father could get a word in edgewise from his spot on the floor, her mother would be off again, pacing among the sleepers, gesticulating as if in the middle of a heated conversation with herself. Once Rosari woke and found her mother kneeling before a statue of the Virgin, and in the morning, as her father and another *paisan* spoke in hushed tones about breakfast, Eleonora stood above Rosari, rocking back and forth as if still aboard the ship, hugging her elbows, and staring with those singed eyes in the direction of a stained-glass window.

Rosari found Italian children to play with on the streets of New York, as well as kids who spoke English and other languages. They communicated through gestures and guesses and a kind of onomatopoeia which bespoke the explosive noises of the new world. They threw snowballs at the noisy motorcars and followed the horse-drawn produce wagons, hoping to snag an apple. They made kissing sounds and pointed at their body parts, grabbed and hit and chased each other whenever they weren't sitting stiff as frozen laundry in the classroom, and occasionally shared a cigarette one of them had stolen from a parent. Among these children she sloughed the end of her name and started referring to herself as Rose, or Rosie.

She read the news sheet she found in front of an Italian bakery, and she tried to read the English primer and newspapers. By the time her parents had found work at sewing machines in the garment district and moved into an apartment with two other families, Rosari was able to read a few hundred words in the new language.

Her mother lasted only two days as a seamstress. The other wives asked her and Rosari to care for the *bambini* in the apartment, an infant named Guido, two toddlers, and four other children aged between three and seven, but the job fell to the girl because her mother kept pacing and leaving the building to walk the snowy streets, ostensibly to hawk oysters with a fishmonger named Piero Balducci.

By spring her mother was a zombie again, sitting most of the day at a table in the noisy apartment, and Rosari was kept out of school to care for the little ones as well as to make sure Eleonora didn't do something harmful to herself or others. Her mother sat still hours on end, but she was known to smack her forehead against the wall, and once she gouged the palm of her hand on purpose with the butcher knife. Her father came home late evenings through slush, cold and weary, his hands barely able to move, and complained to his catatonic wife. He was not a tailor, and neither were the other men in the factory, he said. He just pushed the legs of pantaloons under a machine all day and handed them to the next guy, who sewed cuffs onto them and passed the work to still another guy, and his ears were ringing from the machines, and his lungs were full of catarrh from the cold, and he was sick to death of New York. Rosari was certain that all of these problems were her fault, all the result of a letter she'd written for a man who, in her evening reveries, had broken out of the jail cell in Naples, was currently hiding in a lifeboat on an America-bound freighter, and would come strolling down Mulberry Street some spring day and invite her to sit with him at a sidewalk table for an espresso.

One morning the mother was gone. Lazaro went to work and Rosari cooked for the *bambini* and asked the other mothers, who sold matches and sweet potatoes in the neighborhood, to look for Eleonora while they were on the streets. Word came that evening that she'd run off with Balducci the fishmonger, but by a kind of fire-escape telegraph from building to building Balducci's wife let them know that this was hogwash.

Lazaro left his job to search, once again, for his wife. He and Rosari walked the island of Manhattan and described her to the foodmongers and flower girls on the corners. They cried and wore the soles of their shoes to paper on the streets and asked each other why God would do this sort of thing to them, to Eleonora, to people who had done nothing to deserve misfortune. A week after the disappearance, they came home and knew by the face of the baby's mother that she'd been found.

Father and daughter trudged to the morgue, but only Lazaro was shown the corpse, which had been found naked in the Hudson by the fishermen who supplied Balducci. Never seeing made it impossible for the girl to believe, even after the bleak funeral the church arranged for indigents, even after the river of tears shed by her father and her neighbors. Her mother was merely wandering somewhere, making men's heads turn, stooping over sick children in such beauty as the romances could never describe. Even as an old woman, sitting among the cherry trees behind her California bungalow seventy years later, she would see the breeze toss their blossoms and picture her mother dancing on the snowy deck of the ship, her beautiful mother letting her know, in this way, that she was right: that she had never died.

Without much discussion, the family of two decided it was time to leave again, to look for another new beginning. This time they took to the rails and crossed the North American continent, the swollen rivers and ocean-like prairies, the jagged mountains and frosted deserts. There were Italians working in San Francisco, where it never snowed. There were factories needing men, women, and children with fast hands and strong backs, and rumors of little island neighborhoods where their countrymen sat on the sidewalks and spoke their idiom.

Her father wheezed and slumped over their belongings during most of the journey, a man folding into himself as if preparing for his own death, while she observed the passing world with a certain detachment and imagined her heart encased in the ice of North America. Lazaro seemed too weak to walk on the hilly streets of San Francisco, but somehow they both found work in a leather tannery their first week in California among dozens of other Italians. A year and a half into this miserable job, when Rose had just turned fifteen, they joined a strike, and father and daughter stood among their countrymen while a cavalry of mounted police trotted toward them. After the first screams and deadly blows the crowd scattered, and Rose tried to pull her father along, but he fell and wouldn't get up and told her to leave him there. She knew that his broken heart was no longer strong enough for America, and that the horses would soon crush him, and she cried with impatience, *Papa, get up!* Then she saw a man coming to help, and she thought he was Gratiano, the criminal of her childhood reveries, stooping to support her father. A dark-eyed and agile man, tall and angular in an old-country-style coat and fedora, threw Lazaro over his shoulder and ran as if delivering potatoes to a king. Rosari struggled to keep up with him, the man she would marry later that year, a peasant newly arrived from Calabria named Giuseppe Verbicaro, the man she would have seven children with; and as she ran a sudden breeze came off the bay and tossed her hair loose from its braid, and a sudden heat melted the ice around her heart, and the sound of the horses' hooves faded away, and her lungs filled with the sweet and mischievous air of the new world.

THE IMMACULATE CONCEPTION

Giuseppe

For most of her life, for nearly one hundred years, Rosari referred to 1906 as the year of three catastrophes: the Great San Francisco Earthquake, her father's surrender to catarrh, and her marriage to Giuseppe Verbicaro.

Giuseppe would love and abandon and confound her for fifty years. On the day he rescued her father from the riot police, he carried her heart off as well. He looked a lot like Gratiano the criminal, but there was something forever impenetrable about the man. There was about him the *baciagalupe,* the kiss of the wolf. He was lean and hungry and ferocious as a wolf, but he was loving and gentle, too, when he wanted to be. Who could predict Giuseppe? He was a volcano sleeping one moment, erupting the next.

Unlike her father the barber, unlike herself, Giuseppe had no education and few words. Printed words were like ants on a tablecloth, numbers something you grabbed with the tips of your fingers. He was twice her age when they met, an old wolf prowling strange, foggy hills for food or women, who knew? He worked the leather tannery and he carried towers of baggage and shined shoes in hotels for the rich, and she thought he knew only three or four words in English and maybe only fifty in Italian. In a breadline, the week they met, he was barely able to say, Stew, please.

They married in the courthouse when she was five months pregnant, and lived with her father, who wheezed under his blanket. Their first child, a boy named Giuseppe, was stillborn, and they all wept for two days until the earth split in pieces under their feet, and the city caught fire.

The earthquake made their beds skate and block the door. Rosari, Lazaro, and the Benedetti family, who shared the room, howled as the building swayed like a ship with the escape hatch blocked. By the time they made it outside, Telegraph Hill was on fire.

Giuseppe was shining a rich man's shoes in front of the Majestic Theater on 9th and Market when the seismic convulsion changed his life forever. With a mixture of terror and awe he witnessed the enormous brick edifice, with its roof seventy-five feet above the floor, burst open like a pig on a spit. He stood holding his box of rags and wax as the theater collapsed, as the clay bats missed his head by inches, by a miracle. America was burning and falling around him. God was telling rich and poor alike: He was not pleased.

Rosari never knew that Giuseppe communicated with God because he never mentioned it. He was stoical, conciliatory. The death of his namesake babe was a punishment from the Lord, as was this earthquake. God spoke to Giuseppe in signs, and the destruction of San Francisco was meant to show him by way of example how to make money in America.

Rubble needed to be cleared. Charred and half-toppled houses needed to be demolished to open lots for new buildings. Giuseppe was not a big man, but he became enormous in his strength. He was sinewy and tall for an Italian peasant, and he could swing a sledge-hammer like an ape. He sold the box and shoe wax and became a wrecker.

The city smoldered, the family moved to a basement on Columbus Street, and Giuseppe made money by way of destruction. He attacked houses and toppled them like trees to make room for new construction. He chopped down buildings with a hammer, destroyed banks and offices. He removed the citadels of the rich from the face of the earth, returned the broken towers, wrought of brick and wood, to dust.

And as he worked they had six children, and America went to war with Italy, and wine was illegal to buy. Giuseppe became the father of Narciso, Francesca, Ludovico, Grazia, Mary, and Joe, and he destroyed buildings by day and made wine in his backyard with a cast-iron press by night. He took off for work out of town for months at a time, leaving Rosari to care for the children and the invalid father, who wheezed and barely moved. He wandered and found work and came back with money, rarely telling Rosari what he was about. Whenever he could, he took the oldest boys out of school to clear piles of rubble, but Rosari put her foot down with the youngest. She kept little Joe in class because she knew he had a gift.

The family moved to a house on the Southern Pacific tracks in the East Bay, and Giuseppe planted a garden and bought chickens, rabbits, and a goat. He bought property for fifty dollars at county auctions, worthless swamp that some attorney on the East Coast didn't bother paying the tax on, and his family went without groceries for a month. In Italy, only the wealthy land barons could own property, but in America, Giuseppe was no longer a peasant. With the help of his literate children, he signed ownership contracts, magical documents stamped with gold seals.

The tales of his strength grew among family and neighbors. Giuseppe would break walnuts on his biceps and bend dimes with his teeth. He broke the bones of three men who tried to steal his money in Oakland. There was nothing on earth he couldn't move when he was angry. A family in Richmond, hearing a ferocious noise of growling and shrieking, stepped outside to witness an entire house moving down the street. Giuseppe had jacked it onto skids and was pushing it to a vacant lot.

By the time America went to war again with Italy, Giuseppe's sons had made a business of building instead of wrecking, and he found himself wandering more and more in the hills of San Francisco, drinking with old Italians and listening to God. He often felt directed by God to visit certain places or do certain things, and this was how, somewhere in midcentury, his private thoughts took on strange biblical proportions.

When Giuseppe was seventy-nine years old he decided to marry Maria Guadalupe Diego, a seventeen-year-old prostitute from the Latino barrio of the Mission District. He stepped out of Molinari's on Columbus, a little tipsy, and stood on the steps of the church overlooking Washington Square. This was when he first got the notion that God wanted him to remarry, as he stood on the steps and watched the pigeons circle the spires and fluted alcoves over-head. And even though Giuseppe was currently married, God told him it was time to do it again.

Maria was working North Beach when she spotted Giuseppe shuffling across the park in a forty-year-old, three-piece, pin-striped suit. Two months pregnant by God only knew which salesman from Tulsa or sailor from San Diego, she heard the child speak to her and express its desire to live. This was three days before Mañuel and one of his girls were supposed to take her for the abortion. She lay on the grass in Washington Square watching a cloud the shape of a woman's face while two men played a flute and a clarinet, and the child said, *I want this* from her stomach. *Hijo,* she thought, I need a husband. Some rich old geezer who will leave me alone.

When she approached Giuseppe on the church steps three pigeons hovered inches above his hat and shoulders. Maria began to ask for directions, but laughed unavoidably when the birds landed on the old-timer's hat and shoulders. He shook his head and arms, then found himself laughing, too. A few minutes later they were speaking a mixture of Spanish, Italian, and pidgin English, punctuated by Giuseppe's extreme chivalry.

My wife has passed away, he lied in Italian because this was what God probably wanted him to say. As he brushed a tear from his eye, his gold-plated wristwatch flashed.

I am so very sorry for you, she lied in Spanish. She wore a white dress and leather sandals. A blue rebozo draped her head and shoulders. The consoling touch of her small hand on his was no more than that of a feather.

Giuseppe's wife of more than fifty years, Rosari, was informed of the bigamy by their daughter Francesca, a week after the marriage.

They even got his birth date in Calabria, Francesca said. She leaned over the *Chronicle,* which was spread across her broad lap. Look at that, Ma. It can't be him. You think it's him? Or else somebody found his ID in some saloon?

Rosari pulled on the hem of her black dress. The two women sat facing the street, on the porch of the family house in the East Bay. They were silent for some time. Then Rosari said, Well, that cuts it. Enough is enough.

Giuseppe's children and grandchildren were astounded by his September romance across the bay. It wasn't just embarrassing, even disgusting when you actually thought about it, but wasn't it also illegal? they asked each other. You think they check the records on people? You think in San Francisco they care if an old goat marries a child? In San Francisco?

Who is this little gold brick? Who is this home-wrecker? Francesca shrieked.

I thought Pop was the home-wrecker, her older brother, Narciso, answered.

Precisely where Maria came from was unclear, but it was said she had family who tended sheep and rainy farmland for a land baron in the red-and-green mountains in the Oaxaca department of Mexico. Her older brother had sneaked into California with her and died from a foot infection soon after. The *curandera* who attended the ailing boy with herbs and incantations realized a week before his death that there was nothing to be done to keep him alive, and she told Maria this on a fog-shrouded summer morning on Valencia Street, stirring instant coffee at the card table. The girl, then only fourteen, decided that afternoon that she would have to become a prostitute in order to survive.

She was dark and exquisite, even at that age, with deep eyes which flowed into a fierce anger and then, instantly, ebbed into the sorrow of a confused child. Hustling for a dope peddler named Mañuel near hotels, bars, and nightclubs in North Beach cost her the little affection and sympathy she'd had from neighboring women. She endured their vitriol, avoided their church and markets, and slept frequently in unlocked cars. Her hatred of men, of their rankness and animal minds, almost matched the disgust she felt toward the small, elegant body she was trapped inside of.

A woman who also worked Broadway and North Beach found Maria's marriage to Giuseppe the funniest thing she'd seen in years, but Maria saw little humor in the undertaking. She listened to the need of the child inside her. To Giuseppe she was a virgin and remained so, in spite of the pregnancy, throughout their years together.

It may have been senility. It may have been the overwhelming purity of her beauty in his eyes. Some of the family attributed it to vermouth and closed the book there. Regardless, Giuseppe had not felt such harmony with the world around him, the eucalyptus trees and junipers, the carved stones, the gleam of oil on the bay at dusk, for as long as memory. And God had often dealt Giuseppe a mysterious hand, giving him bread for destruction instead of craft, making him appear the rake in the bars and social clubs of Little Italy with a wife conveniently stirring pots across the bay when, as He and Giuseppe only knew, he'd been struck impotent some twenty years earlier after an injury and a disgusting encounter in the Tenderloin. And now God had told Giuseppe Verbicaro, brittle-boned old sinner with a limp sex, drinker and dreamer with a big fedora and wandering brogans, to provide for this angel.

Maria's cappuccino-colored skin, her sudden laughter and eyes black as midnight, made him smile like a baby. The smell of her hair was from another world. So when she informed him that she was with child, about two months after the courthouse wedding, he asked simply how and by whom. She answered with a steady voice: *Dios sabe* and *Nadie*. God knows. Nobody.

He accepted the miracle. Maybe he remembered the story, told by another Italian shoe shine before the earthquake, about a woman in the old Sutro Baths at the Cliff House. Sperm, thrashing madly upstream in public pools, could make things unsafe for women anywhere outside their own bathrooms. Maybe he took it the way he received the columns of sunlight finding him through morning fog on a long walk to the liquor store on Grant, as something too beautiful to ask questions about.

One night he decided that God had slipped between Maria's thighs while she slept and planted His seed with a penis as thin as a thread of gold. God's penis was incredibly thin, but it was also unbelievably long. It stretched through the open window of their flat on Green Street, past the top of the Coit Tower; it reached down from the sky, where a full moon hung beside it like a testicle filled with celestial semen. Giuseppe chuckled as he found his way to the toilet in the dark. God has only one ball, he said to himself.

The marriage turned out better than Maria had expected, due in large part to Giuseppe's impotence, but also to his generosity. He gave her money for nice clothes and food, for movies and tickets to the Funhouse and Playland at the beach. He watched her make dolls out of cornhusks and yarn. That first summer, learning that she craved fresh cherries, he walked a few miles with her to the Japanese Tea Garden and picked his fedora full amid bonsai maples and miniature pagodas.

In many respects she was still a child, coerced at an early age into selling her body and her childhood. A pimp named Mañuel had seen her potential and made her a lucrative product. He injected her with drugs, raped and sodomized her, beat her with his fists until she thought of the dark water and the peace of falling from the Golden Gate. It was the unborn infant who saved her, who gave her a reason to find a way to live.

News of the pregnancy put the frosting on Giuseppe's disgrace. What could there be under the sun to shock and disgust you more than this? his children wanted to know. But the birth inspired a sea change. Without plan or announcement his daughters and grandchildren came to Green Street with gifts, with ravioli and a whole salmon and fig cookies for the mother, with a flannel bunting and bibs for the baby. They held the child and marveled at his beautiful skin, the same as his mother's, at his perfect oval face and black eyes. They took Maria shopping at Macy's and made her eat so her hips and breasts could get bigger. Francesca's daughter Susan struggled to understand Maria's Spanish, even the name of her son. Hey-Zeus, you call him?

Sí, Jesús, she replied.

He's a little miracle, that's for sure.

They babysat while Maria went to the Funhouse and flew down the wooden slide on a potato sack or lost herself among the mirrors. They scolded Giuseppe for being a skinflint, and they threw out his liquor bottles. They shook their heads and sighed, imagining the old man's faux virility. They walked around the kitchen holding the little miracle to their breasts, singing old show tunes.

One morning between three and four Giuseppe had trekked out of bed to the toilet when he heard a rattling. Somebody was trying the door. He stood behind it a moment, then cleared his throat. The rattling stopped.

Hey, Giuseppe whispered. He thought it might be old Desiderio, locked out for the night by his angry wife. *Che cosa?*

A man's voice on the other side spoke in English and Spanish. He said he was Maria's family. Giuseppe opened the door.

The fellow was young with slicked-back hair, and he kept sniffing like he had a cold. Giuseppe made espresso. The two men tiptoed around the kitchen to Maria's bedroom door, where they could see mother and babe sleeping. The man sniffed and chuckled. His hands and eyes moved constantly. They returned to the kitchen.

Giuseppe pulled the salmon, two feet long and stiff as a plank, from the icebox and placed it in a pan to thaw. He moved slowly, as if most of his joints were as frozen as the fish, crushing garlic and basil leaves into a bowl. The young man asked why in the hell Maria had chosen him to fleece. Giuseppe didn't understand his English. There was a pistol, shiny as tinsel, in the young man's hand. This he understood. What the fuck did this *anciano* think he was doing? Ancient old man in pajamas holding a fish.

In the old stories, in the Good Book which Giuseppe couldn't read, the Lord made a man and a woman and kicked them out of paradise for being nosy. Later, in Giuseppe's recollection, He sent a child to save us all. It was a strange plan when you thought about it. He gets with child a virgin, then appoints some old man to look after them.

The young man said he needed Maria because she brought it in fast and because nobody ducks out on him. He laughed. You can buy it on the street next week, if I don't kill you.

The gun barrel was less than a yard from Giuseppe's face. The flat was silent, save the ticking of a clock and the occasional bleating of ships on the bay. Giuseppe wondered what God might have up His sleeve. Was it time for him to die? Was it time for Maria and her little miracle to die? And at that moment the little miracle screamed.

It was a scream like an ice pick in the head, like a siren to wake the dead out of hell. The young man covered his ears, and Giuseppe made like his old hero, DiMaggio, clearing the bases at Seals Stadium. He made like he was bringing down the house with one swing, with a fish as his hammer. The man's shiny head cracked like a walnut against the door frame. Blood seeped from his ears and mouth. Maria knelt and picked up the pistol. *Gracias,* she whispered to Giuseppe.

He fitted into a large burlap potato sack, but it took both of them to carry him to the pier. Already the produce trucks were arriving with their many gifts from the fields and valleys of California, with dates and avocados, with oranges bright as the sun from the south. And the child on his mother's hip pointed the way, singing in his own tongue as Maria and Giuseppe slouched under the weight of our world and trudged through the darkness to the water.

THE PENNY ARCADE

Joe

Joe would have been Giuseppe but for his mother's trick. Giuseppe and Rosari Verbicaro's first child, whom they'd named after his father, had died when delivered from the womb. The old midwives were as confused and distraught as the mother, and they searched their brains for reasons. Rosari was too young, perhaps. Rosari didn't drink enough wine or nanny-goat milk. The mother had her own theory, which had to do with the name and the smoldering temper of her husband, and she insisted on giving the second, also a boy, his own name. He grew to be a beautiful but slow-witted lad, and Rosari succeeded in giving birth to five more after him, three girls and two boys, the last of which Giuseppe demanded to tag his name onto. Rosari nodded, but when the time came for signing the certificate, she smiled and wrote the name *Joe*.

By this time, English had invaded the household vernacular of all but the old man, and the children preferred calling the baby Joe, anyway. It took Giuseppe a few years to catch on. He sat at the table after a day of backbreaking work, stewed on homemade wine, while the children were laughing and fighting over the last serving of string beans. When he asked what the boy's name was, Giuseppe or Joe, Rosari said, in Italian, What's it to you, old-timer? It worked.

Joe's brothers and sisters were all taken out of school in order to work, either to haul debris for the old man or to sew at some sweatshop, but Rosari kept her youngest in class because she recognized his shrewd mind. Little Joe had a better head for math than his elementary school teachers. He discovered the Fibonacci sequence on his own, the wonderful pyramid of relationships, while doodling in his notebook during grammar. He stared at ceilings and buildings and calculated the dimensions, the number of joists and beams in the school. He figured probabilities for an illiterate bookmaker at the dog track when he was ten, the numbers tumbling inside his brain while he groomed and walked the whippets after school, and was given a nickel for his efforts.

He was adorable and bossy in the way that only the youngest can be, the baby that Mama protects and defends before the rest of the brood, and he was a shrimp and a know-it-all who was usually right. He hated his family's poverty, which forced him to wear all the hand-me-downs, even his sisters' shoes, to school, and determined to make piles of money when he grew up. When he got teased he lashed out with his fists, and he was a scrapper. He once broke a boy's nose for saying the word *ravioli*.

Ranking next to poverty was shame for his family heritage. He watched the newsreels and movies in which Italians were happy idiots who played the concertina and drank wine like his pop, and he dreamed of being a famous inventor with a nose job and a penthouse in San Francisco. Joe thought of changing his last name, too, especially for business purposes. Joe Verb: Action Enterprises. But the business Joe eventually steered was a family affair, a group of hungry Italians building, first on the swamp his father had bought for next to nothing, and later anywhere Uncle Sam asked them to, during the war boom of the '40s.

By the late '50s, Joe and his brothers and sisters, whose husbands worked for the family business, were doing well, but they thought their father had lost his mind. He'd always been a drinker and wanderer, and had often spent months away from home at jobs with other Italians or just hanging out in the island culture of North Beach, but now his brain had stepped off a cliff, and at the bottom of that cliff was a teenaged hooker and her illegitimate baby.

No ugly stereotyping could have disgusted Joe more than these latest shenanigans, no joke about Italian soldiers or Italian funerals with only two pallbearers could have angered him further. He looked at himself in the barber's mirror and asked for a flattop; he avoided Italian food, except on Sundays at his mother's; he hid the Sinatra records under a stack of magazines until his daughter Penny found them and filled the house with Frankie Boy swinging with Nelson Riddle's band.

It was Penny who talked him into going to see the old man. They were at a little Italian hole in the wall celebrating her twelfth birthday, just daddy and daughter, and she brought the subject up as if it had just occurred to her. Isn't Grandpa's place a few blocks from here? Shouldn't we drop in on them?

Why? Joe glared at the menu.

You've got to see that baby, Dad. He is so beautiful! Your, um . . . brother, Jesús.

Maria, the young Mexican mother who pronounced Jesús like *Hey-Zeus,* fascinated Penny as much as the baby did. Giuseppe, the butt of a thousand jokes in Rosari's repertoire, was a harmless geezer to his granddaughter, a funny old guy who would probably slip her a five-dollar bill as a birthday present.

They'd taken the L train from Berkeley over the Bay Bridge and a cable car to Chinatown, from which they'd walked to North Beach. A waiter spoke to Joe in Italian, and Joe reminded the guy that they were in America, if he didn't notice. Joe checked his watch, tapped his fingers on the table, made notations on a napkin. He had a hell of a lot on his mind because his brothers were watching the shop and an important deal was imminent, but he wanted to give Penny her day. He left the table to call Ludovico, read him some numbers from the napkin, and told Lu to take them down, but his brother, whose moods were sudden and violent, told him to butt the hell out and enjoy his daughter and his ravioli, for Christ's sake.

Try prime rib, Joe said. You sure you guys are all right? These bastards from New Jersey will have your peter in their pocket the minute you shake hands, Lu.

Hey, what are we, a bunch of rubes? You think we just got off the banana boat?

Giuseppe's flat in Little Italy reminded Joe of the poverty he'd escaped and kept from his children: clothes on the lines between buildings, peppers and garlic hanging not far from them, loud voices yelling from one stoop to the next, broken glass and strong smells of urine and garbage in the alleyway. There was an old Mexican woman in the flat, and she said that *la familia* had gone to the beach. Joe laughed and thanked God. He fairly danced down the steps and the steep sidewalks to the streetcar stop with his daughter, calculating the time it would take to get her home and himself to the business. Penny reminded him that they were going to the Natural History Museum next. The what? The place with the alligators. He'd promised.

Christ. Joe hated it: waiting on the corner, squeezing in with all those people, rocking up and down the hills while the Jersey deal might be going down. They were stuck in a jam for fifteen minutes, and the siren of an ambulance announced the reason for the delay. Penny opened the bus window and stuck her head out as the attendants hustled with the stretcher, and Joe scolded her for snooping. Her eyes and mouth were open with wonder. Penny, you get back in your seat this minute, he hissed, and her face colored as she obeyed.

It was a mild summer afternoon in the city, fresh with strands of fog drifting among the buildings and the sunny eucalyptus and Monterey pines of the park. Joe and his daughter walked through the grove of pollarded sycamores to the museum and found the building closed. Penny suggested they walk to the beach and Playland.

Walk? Joe asked. On purpose?

It's only a mile or so, I think.

Christ, Penny, only a goddamned idiot would walk clear from here to the beach. Excuse my French.

Then I must be a goddamned idiot, the girl said. She wore a

summery dress and saddle shoes, and a new alpaca sweater was draped over her shoulders to ward off the pockets of fog and sea breeze. Joe figured that more loot had been spent on this one outfit than his entire wardrobe from age one to nineteen, and she kept growing out of things. Already her legs were nearly as long as his, her stride brisk and determined. They passed the lake with the pedal boats, crossed a polo field big as a goddamned aircraft carrier, muddied Joe's best shoes near a creek. He saw a booth and told her to wait a minute while he got on the horn again. Narciso answered.

Ciso, what's up? Did the guys from Jersey call?

They're here, Joe. They're real nice guys.

Oh, Christ. Joe's stomach turned, and he asked to talk with his other brother, Ludovico. Penny was feeding French bread to a group of noisy ducks right next to the booth.

Joe, Narciso said after a bit, Lu says it's all taken care of. It's fine, Joe. These are great guys. How's little Penny?

Jesus Christ, Ciso, of course they're nice guys, they're about to ask us to drop our pants and spread our legs. Get Lu.

There was a long pause. The ducks snapped at Penny's legs, and she shrieked happily. Joe could hear voices, laughter, maybe a radio broadcast of a ballgame, a man saying the word *southpaw*. Then Sammy, the bookkeeper from the Philippines: Hello? Is somebody on the line?

Get me Lu, Sam, right now.

Oh, hey, Mr. Verbicaro! Hey, I'm sorry. He and Ciso just took off with these guys for lunch.

Son of a goddamned bitch. Joe slammed the receiver so hard the ducks bolted.

A s they neared the shore the fog assaulted them. It rolled through the cypress and over the grass, tumbling against itself like an avalanche. The amusement park glowed and squawked somewhere in those snowy depths, its tacky music and Christmas lights beckoning like a buried city of sin which God had failed to destroy. Every foolish pleasure from the '20s and the turn of the century, gartered legs, beer foaming the underside of handlebar mustaches, flapper dresses, wheels of fortune, and penny arcades, was depicted in garish colors which, though blasted by years of weather and generations of children, beamed at Joe through the fog as he approached.

Penny wanted to go to the Funhouse first, and they stood in line before the mechanical hag, the laughing, wild-haired, freckle-faced old woman in the booth. Joe fumed about his brothers, his father, and, to some degree, his willful daughter, who had dragged him to this spot, in bitter fog, before this ugly, guffawing woman. Her head rocked back when she let loose with the biggest laughs, and her arms in the wild striped sleeves jerked like a spastic's. It made Joe wonder about laughter itself for the first time in his life; it made it suspect in his mind. What a miserable thing it was, really, a desperate and mindless noise. What an ugly animal sound, imbued with nothing nobler than retching or ejaculating.

Daddy, where are you? Penny shrieked and laughed, lost some-

where before him in the house of mirrors. Joe's anger was like his
father's, slow-building, deadly, filled with resentment and purpose.
His brother Lu would explode at the slightest provocation and
laugh a moment later, and Narciso's fuse was so long it might circle
the earth twice before a wisp of smoke could be seen on the hori-
zon, but Joe banked his logs in silence toward a coming forest fire.
He stepped slowly through the house of mirrors while children
squeezed past him, shrieking black and brown and yellow and white
kids giggling and yelling, and felt the familiar blood of injustice beat
in his throat. He came to the junctures in the maze of reflections
and locked eyes with the man in front of him, this idiot with the
crew cut and monkey suit, and wanted to punch his own lights out.
Which way? He asked the many images of himself. I don't have time
to screw around. Kids were swirling past him in each direction.

Daddy, are you still in there? He could hear Penny's voice above
the din of laughter and yelling. I'll meet you at the base of the slide,
she yelled. Jesus Christ on a goddamned pogo stick, Joe muttered
when he came to another dead end. A boy behind him laughed and
said, You hear that guy?

He had no inkling what the hell people found amusing about
getting lost. Penny was probably ten yards from him, and he had to
navigate through a maze five times that length. If the monster in the
myth, the guy with the bull's head, were waiting for him around the
next bend, Joe would be ready to break his nose.

Penny called to him again, and he was so mad he didn't answer.
By now Joe had his pen out and was making tabulations on the palm

of his hand, five panels, left turn, three panels, right turn. Children zoomed past him. He was surrounded by facets of himself, the angry boy, the embarrassed boy, the lost boy; the little mathematician so poor he lacked a piece of paper, the little Italian kid in his sister's saddle shoes. He stood in sight of the entrance, the fog, the laughing hag's booth, back at the goddamned beginning, and swore. He turned and saw himself in a panel, mouth open in confusion, pen poised above his palm. Somebody yanked his coat.

You lost, mister? a boy with black, curly hair, younger than Penny, asked him in Italian. Follow me.

Joe followed the boy and was through the mirrors and in the center of the Funhouse in two minutes. He gave the kid four bits. The kid stuffed the quarters into his baggy dungarees and raced off.

The open center of the Funhouse smelled like an old gymnasium, like dirty socks and stinky shoes and the pine-scented wax and cleansers used on the hardwood floor. Penny was flying down the enormous wooden slide on a potato sack, her black hair and her petticoat sweeping back, her mouth open in a huge smile. When she got to the bottom she grabbed a girl by the wrist and dragged her over to Joe.

Dad, she yelled, her face flushed and damp, guess who this is!

The girl was nearly a young woman, and although Joe was a straight shooter and teetotaler compared to his brothers, he knew enough about the blue-light district to guess this girl had been around. She was beautiful and dark, to be sure, but there was something tawdry about her, something in her eyes, which had street

corners in them, some odor of desperation, of drugs or booze. I
don't know who this is, Joe said. And I don't want you to hang
around somebody like this, he said to himself.

His daughter laughed. Dad, this is Maria!

Who?

Your stepmom!

The young woman shook his hand, then gestured for them to
wait before she darted off. Penny ran once through an obstacle
course of rolling barrels and tipping boards while Joe pictured his
old man in the labyrinth of mirrors, a lusty, snorting, white-haired
monster with booze on his breath and goat horns sprouting out of
his skull. He imagined how he might scare the children, and how
some boy like the little guy who'd just guided Joe through the mirrors might trip the old man into a glass panel or jump on his back
and strangle him. Maria and Penny were talking, as much with
hands as with words, near the giant barrel while Joe mused about
Giuseppe. Penny ran to him.

Grandpa's lost! She tugged on Joe's arm.

So what else is new?

He took off with the baby!

Giuseppe had been getting lost on a routine basis. Penny told Joe
about an afternoon spent with Aunt Francesca and Cousin Susan
hunting all over Little Italy, down Columbus Street to Washington
Square and the boccie courts, to the liquor stores in Chinatown,

and finally finding him at the wharf staring at the water. Joe wanted to know why in the hell this young mother had left the baby with an old drunk whose brain had one foot on a banana peel, but he couldn't navigate her Spanish. They jogged through the carnival crowd, under the Ferris wheel, which turned slowly and disappeared in fog, among the dart-throwing and ring-tossing booths, then into the huge arcade. Joe remembered putting a penny into one of the old machines many years ago, cranking the handle until he saw, in a jerky, magical dance of white flesh against a black background, his first glimpse of a naked woman.

They crossed the highway to the beach. The fog lifted, swept to the south like wind-tossed hair, and the sudden gleam of sunlight made Joe squint. Penny saw them first and pointed, across the slick plane of sand which disappeared in fog, at the tiny, smoky figures of a man in a fedora and a toddler holding his hand. The old goat was moving stiffly, and the child's shiny black hair bounced in the wind. Penny and Maria stepped over the garbage and driftwood and kicked off their shoes while Joe sat on the seawall and looked at his watch. He yelled to Penny that he needed to make another phone call pretty soon, and she called back that they'd be on the beach with Grandpa.

Don't get your clothes wet, he yelled. Something stank, a dead seal or some bum's turd buried in the sand, and he stepped down to the beach and walked over to a log upwind. He imagined that his brothers were probably drunk and laughing while a bunch of sleazy bastards put their business in the shitcan. He imagined his father having sex with a teenaged whore, the woman dancing around in the surf with his daughter. The girls raised their skirts high above their knees while the water foamed around them.

He crushed a crab shell under his heel and hurled a stone at a log. He picked up a shell and observed it among the tabulations he'd made on his palm in the house of mirrors. Joe imagined some hermit crab had once lived in it, and wondered how the hell a crab could build a house like that, then realized that the crab had probably just found it and taken it the way his old man had snagged neglected land from lazy investors for next to nothing. But something built it, he said to himself, some little shellfish, and as he studied the perfect spiral he thought how somebody might explain its design with a series of triangles, a progression of right triangles, the hypotenuse of one becoming the base of the next. He held the shell, closed his eyes, and as he took in the scent of the briny air he returned in memory to the arcade from childhood, the secret peepshow world in the machine. That distant afternoon when he'd chased friends up and down this same beach and seen the woman in the box was linked somehow to looking into the heart of the shell today.

His daughter was still lifting her knees in the foam, her black hair tossed back and bouncing, and his father and the baby were trudging in the opposite direction now, along the water's edge, their distant shapes silhouetted against the radiant mist. Joe turned and brushed the sand from his trousers.

The arcade was dark after the shore's brilliance, and it took a moment for his eyes to read the signs. He got change from a cigar-smoking boy in a booth and scanned the dark recesses for a phone. Sammy answered and said that his brothers were still out with New

Jersey. The carousel started up as he spoke, and it was hard to hear him. Joe watched the horses moving up and down. Could they do any damage without his signature? Sammy didn't see how they could, and Joe agreed.

Several kids were at pinball, but none at the ancient penny arcade machines (which now demanded a nickel), and as Joe strolled among them he realized that the boy had given him twenty nickels for his buck, and he had eighteen left, and his brothers probably couldn't do anything without his signature, so what the hell. He glanced up and down the aisles of dusty machines, sighed, and dropped a nickel into one of them.

A little man with a bushy mustache was crank-starting a car. Joe could adjust the speed of the jerky black and white images with his arm, and he found it amusing that he and the man were cranking handles simultaneously, the ghost of an actor who died years ago and Joe moving their right arms in perfect sync. When the man hopped into the jalopy, the fenders fell off. Joe shook his head and peered up and down the aisles sheepishly. He wondered if he could find it or if it had long since been replaced.

He peeped into a few more machines. On some the metal visor above the eye sockets was worn smooth and shiny. The actors in the little films were obscure, the scenes taken from all manner of unsuccessful projects and experiments with the moving picture craft. Physical comedy, pratfalls, smoke and combustion were the main fare, but there were several very odd pieces: men rowing boats and lifting dumbbells, soldiers marching like wind-up toys. He had three nickels left when he found it.

The tiny figure in profile was running in place, the muscles of her hip moving to the rhythm of Joe's arm, her small breasts bouncing with the sway of Joe's shoulder. She was so small and naked, so white and vulnerable jogging before the pitch-black backdrop, her long hair pinned on top of her head. Her eyes looked frightened or startled, and Joe's heart pounded as he cranked the handle. The screen went black.

He dropped another coin and moved more slowly this time, and still again more slowly with his last nickel. When he finished and started out of the semi-open, cavernous building he felt beads of sweat dribble down his dress shirt. He stood above the gleaming ocean feeling a bit foolish and ashamed.

Penny and Maria were in almost the precise place they'd been when Joe had left, silhouettes moving in the radiant mist, wading in the surf. Joe shuffled toward them and peered down the beach for the old man. A good fifty yards south of the girls the toddler crouched and bounced atop a log, but Giuseppe was nowhere in sight. Damn that old goat, Joe said to himself, leaving a child alone by the water. He started for Jesús. Obviously, the girls hadn't seen the old man disappear. The toddler walked on the log and pulled something off one end of it. Then he ran west, across the smooth expanse of sand, clutching something round and floppy. Kelp? Jellyfish? No: the object left the boy's hand and rode the wind a moment like a cartoon spacecraft before it landed on the wet sand. It was a fedora.

Joe ran, too, but he slipped in soft sand and bit his tongue. He knew it was his father who lay motionless, looking from this perspective more like driftwood washed ashore than a man, and that the child was heading for the receding water. The girls heard him yell and stared at him. Joe hadn't run for years, not since a charity ballgame, and as he lifted his legs he thought of the little naked woman running in place, how the muscles of her hip flexed. He thought how she'd been filmed in some clinical setting and possibly against her will, like a Jewess studied by Nazi doctors, and he realized that he had always held a secret love for her, for her beauty as well as her vulnerability. Baby Jesús ran with his arms out, as if to embrace the water, and Joe could see that a large wave was coming, green and gleaming like a polished stone, just starting to crest and tumble toward the child, and Joe lifted his knees and pumped his arms and legs as hard as he could.

The toddler disappeared underwater a moment before Joe ran into the frigid ocean. A black ball, more like a sea palm than the head of a child, popped above the foam. Jesús's beautiful brown face rose above the surface of the wave, as if the sea were debating whether to take the baby or deliver him. The water knocked Joe down once, but he regained his feet. His good suit dripped and poured from the pockets, his best loafers got sucked off his feet and swallowed. He stumbled and crept in waist-high surf, and the boy floated into his arms.

The water hissed up to Giuseppe as well and soaked his old flannel shirt and khaki trousers. Joe, still up to his thighs in water, saw Maria struggling toward him, her dress soaked and clinging to her body, and in the distance Penny turning the old man onto his back because the water had covered his face. The baby wheezed and spewed seawater, the mother shrieked and staggered with arms out-stretched, and Joe could see his daughter stooped beside his father. He handed Jesús to Maria and held her elbow as they trudged to shore.

Penny leaned above her grandfather the way she'd stand while examining the rocks and tidal pools, the way she'd lean on the rail other days to gaze down at the alligators. Daddy, is he, she asked, is he, is he? Before kneeling to examine him Joe already knew that his fa-ther was gone, knew as much as he'd known anything in his life that the drunk old goat, the *paisano* who'd followed sheep into the Cal-abrian hills, had finally wandered off where nobody could find him.

He could see that his daughter was taking this in, was recording in her mind the look of the corpse of the old tyrant, an artifact no more alive than a sarcophagus or a piece of petrified wood. He knelt and touched the place where a jugular should tap back, brushed his fingers across the old man's cheek and ear, and thought of the heart of the shell and the arcade, of that moment when the design, maybe the intent, of a mystery is revealed.

Giuseppe's eyes and mouth were open; flecks of water and mica glittered in his whiskers like stars. Joe opened his mouth and wept for the first time since childhood. He begged God's pardon that both he and his daughter must stare into the private chambers as Penny clung to his shoulder and wailed. He asked forgiveness that they must trespass on others' grief and feed their eyes again and again.

THE APPLES OF THE EARTH

Jesús

Maria and her son, Jesús, had to flee the pimps and collectors of San Francisco after the old man died. Giuseppe's family argued among themselves about their obligation to the girl, a teenaged hooker without a mother or father of her own. The women offered babysitting and a pool of cash, saying that the girl deserved a hand, whether or not the baby was of their blood. Giuseppe's sons Ludovico and Joe knew that the smart money said he wasn't.

A few months after the funeral Maria was approached at a produce market in Chinatown by a prostitute who'd worked with her four years earlier. It was this conversation with Lin, the Chinese hooker, along with a profound fatalism in Maria's soul, which tipped her back into the oldest profession and the addictive powders that sustained her.

She would leave the toddler with Giuseppe's granddaughters or with an old Mexican woman named Rosanidia and sit on the laps of drunk businessmen on Broadway. One of them turned out to be the bill collector hired by her landlord, a Neapolitan nickel-and-dime

thug named Paolo who proposed marriage daily and professed torment when he saw her sitting on other men. The fire of love in his
heart was often translated into punching and kicking, and Maria
found herself weeping one morning with a broken jaw, shaking like
an epileptic, craving cocaine and imagining the many ways she
should end her life. But not now, God seemed to say to her, because
the child needed her.

The next day she took Jesús and a duffel bag to Rosanidia's flat
in the Mission District. There she hid and rode out the drug nausea
while her jaw healed. It took two months for the various men with
financial and romantic interests to find her, but by then Rosanidia
had a plan.

The old woman's nephew had a friend named José, a migrant
farm worker who traveled alone. The man had a wife and seven
children in Chihuahua that Rosanidia didn't know about. The
nephew just said he was lonely and had tender feelings for Maria,
whom he'd never spoken to, but whose loveliness would be appar-
ent to a blind armadillo.

They took off in José's station wagon for the Salinas Valley and
picked artichokes. José's hands were swift and strong, and it didn't
take them long to find their way under Maria's skirt as they lay in
the *patron*'s shack with Jesús sleeping an arm's length away. Maria
tried to push him away, but no word or gesture of discouragement
could stop José from forcing himself on her. After he was done, she
told him, God has a dark plan for you and for me, and laughed. José
lay panic-stricken in the musty one-room shack, wondering if this

woman were a witch or possessed by an evil spirit. A few hours later, unable to sleep, he slipped out to his station wagon.

Of God's dark plan Jesús was also aware because his mother spoke of it often, even as she worked the rows of artichokes and lettuce in the heat of midday. The foundation of her apocalyptic vision may have come from the priests of her childhood in the tropical mountains of Oaxaca, in a primarily Indian community still darkened by the shadow of colonial oppression, or it may have come from the deaths of her parents and brother which had led to her childhood prostitution in San Francisco's Mission District. She said it came from God's mouth itself because she heard His voice in her head on a daily basis, and generally He was not pleased with things. Jesús understood God's dark plan to involve mass destruction and wholesale death, the ocean suddenly tumbling over the Gabilan Mountains and filling the valley they were in, the city of San Francisco falling and burning magnificently. He understood it to require the presence of various tools of the devil, men whose hearts were possessed or turned to stones as cold as the river cobbles he struck with his hoe while working alongside his mother, to tempt and torment the few righteous souls on God's earth.

It wasn't surprising then that little Jesús, toddling the rows barefoot with his straw sombrero and broken hoe, spotted the evil man before the others who stooped in the field. Paolo stood on the dirt road beside the irrigation ditch, and Jesús ran to tell his mother. The collector had been searching the Salinas Valley all day after he had convinced old Rosanidia, by way of breaking her finger and burning her cheek with a cigar, to give him an idea where to find the woman he loved. He stood in the mountain shadows of late afternoon wearing a dark suit and dark glasses, smoking, nodding his head. Maria called to José, and another man ran for the *patron*.

The *patron* was an obese Argentine who carried a shotgun for the gophers and snakes, and this he leveled at Paolo, who backed away. Maria watched the collector gesture with his arms while the *patron* marched him down the irrigation road to his shiny car. The car didn't leave immediately, though. Maria could feel Paolo watching her from behind its windshield. A couple of men stacking pallets went up to the driver's window, and it looked like the collector handed something to one of these men. Later, after the car had gone, a boy handed Maria a box of chocolates, in which she found a ten-dollar bill and these words, written in a mishmash of Italian and Spanish: *Maria, Every night I lie in a torment of love for you. Please come back. I will treat you like a queen because I love you more than I love my own mother. Your Paolo.*

Maria convinced José that they needed to clear out that night, and a few other farm workers followed their station wagon north. They picked apples outside Hood River, Oregon, and this was the first vision of snow for mother and son, from a tall, three-legged ladder in the apple trees where Mount Hood filled the sky. These were days of beauty for her, the ache of the ladder pressing on the soles of her feet and the shape of apples in her hands. The sensation remained in her bones and in her dreams at night, along with the volcano which gleamed above her like a loving face. Jesús would eat the sweet fallen fruit and talk with her while she worked in the dappled light, and they would collapse in a sweet sort of apple-scented exhaustion at night, left alone in the wall tent while José slept in the car, a world away from the evil of the city.

They worked their way east to the sugar beets along the Snake River, dry country with little to see beyond the grain elevators and distant peaks until nightfall, when the sky filled with stars and the creamy brush strokes of the galaxy. Maria and Jesús wondered about the enormous silo dug into the river clay like the grave of a giant, and were told by the rancher's wife, a ruddy-faced French-woman, that it held *earth apples* by the millions. This excited the child, the idea of apple trees growing in some land deep within the earth, and Maria teased Jesús in a friendly way and encouraged his fantasy.

One windy afternoon in the beet fields Maria felt a chill and looked to see a boy staring at her. In that moment she knew several things which God had planned: that this boy had accepted more than chocolate from Paolo in Salinas, that the bill collector would come soon, and that blood would be shed. She told José that they needed to leave again, that night, and he refused because payday was the following Friday. Woman, he said, you believe too much in dark signs. He resumed work, but crossed himself first.

The next day there was a heavy frost on the beets and sage-brush. Maria worked all day with a chill in her right shoulder as she swung her machete. Even at midday she was cold enough to leave the poncho on as she worked. A sour wind, filled with the stink of a potato-processing plant, swept the fields.

Once again, Jesús saw the evil men in their dark suits and ran to tell his mother. Paolo was accompanied this time by a huge, dim-witted thug named Anastácio Váldez. They walked among the beet rows laughing softly, striding with the confidence of landowners. It was near sunset, and their shadows stretched across the rows as they made their way to Maria and her child.

Paolo sang a few lyrics from a popular doo-wop song of the times, a song about crossing mountains and valleys to get to the woman he loved, while Tacho Valdez laughed. Then the Neapolitan spread his arms, inviting Maria to embrace him. Maria stepped back.

It puzzled Tacho, as he put it to Maria in his street Spanish, that she would prefer digging in shit like a pig to a life of luxury in the city with a rich man like Paolo who loved her. She stood with dried mud dusting her bare feet and legs, her hands scratched by thistles and leaves and callused by work, and described the punishment that God had in store for them. This made both men laugh. By now José and three other men had gathered in the dusky light near Maria and her child. Paolo shrugged and pulled a stiletto from his pocket. Tacho produced a length of chain.

Former zoot-suiters who'd cut their teeth breaking thumbs for the mob, Paolo and Tacho were accustomed to frightening the poor country Mexicans in the barrio with a gesture or a threat. While Paolo brandished his knife Tacho explained how much he and the mafioso next to him enjoyed breaking bones and performing vari-ous acts of castration and vivisection on little *indios* such as them. Although Paolo didn't understand all of the monologue, he got the gist of the Spanish insults and chuckled. What neither he nor Tacho knew was that every campesino, from age five onward, wielded a machete with breathtaking authority. Country folk like Maria used the tool from childhood in order to chop firewood, harvest crops, slaughter livestock, and separate the heads of vipers from the rest of their bodies.

Paolo grabbed Maria's elbow, and José shoved him, as much to save face in front of his *compañeros* as to defend the woman. The bill collector's stiletto sliced José's throat, and the powerful little man stood holding the gash while blood squirted between his fingers. He stared at Maria before his legs buckled. Then Maria swung the machete from beneath her poncho and buried it in her former lover's leg. A storm of blades and screams followed.

The little drunk *patron* saw the carnage, vomited, and called the rancher. It made sense to both him and his boss to let an entire migrant community take to their heels before calling the authorities. In fact, with payroll a couple of days off, the crisis became an opportunity in disguise from the rancher's perspective. Scare the hell out of them, he suggested.

José died in the arms of his *compañeros* and was left in a trough between two endless rows of beets. The two thugs were so horribly slaughtered that a photo of their dismembered corpses found its way into a *National Enquirer* issue some weeks later, under the caption Crazed Farmworkers Attack Threshing Machine! In the photograph Paolo's eyes seemed to be regarding each other from two separate faces across the mangled expanse of his torso. Parts of Tacho Valdez lay in the dust as if awaiting assembly. A leg punctuated by a laced oxford lay across the big man's neck.

When the *patron* told the workers that an army of immigration and police was on its way, the campesinos scattered All but Maria, who held her child in one hand and the bloody machete in the other, unable to move. The camp grew quiet, the land dark, while she stood holding her child and the blade, waiting for God to complete His celestial thought. God seemed in the middle of an idea of how the woman should kill herself and her child, but He wasn't clear about the details. Should she slit her wrists first? How would He have her end the innocent one's life with the least pain? Should they leap into the river? The Snake curved in the distance, a dull shard of black glass near a warehouse, a dark shape slithering between the fields.

When the sirens sounded Jesús urged his mother to move. Here was where their thoughts diverged, as if a fork in the road of God's mind appeared and the child would always take a different road from his mother's. It even seemed possible, as Maria would see it later, that Jesús was able to convince God to change His mind. Lights bumped along the dirt road near the fenced housing enclosure, swept through the field and smeared across the distant river. Jesús tugged on his mother's hand, and she started, as if awakened from a dream. She walked like a somnambulist, tugged by her child toward the dugout silo more than a mile away, the huge grave where the apples of the earth were stored. They could hear the voices of demons warped by a bullhorn among the shrieks of sirens. The mound at the end of the beet field became a formless sweep of black, an emptiness at the edge of the starry sky.

They entered the place of utter darkness where the *pommes de terre, manzanas de la tierra,* were heaped, and felt their way until they were hidden, half buried among them. To the mother the close darkness, the musty earth odor, and the lumpy, cold potatoes were a taste of the necropolis in God's plans, a city where the corpses of sinners would soon be stacked by the millions. But for the child the tubers were whimsically shaped apples from another world. He knew a hidden orchard lay somewhere farther back, deep within the earth. He knew trees of golden fruit gleamed in a light not of this world.

THE MAGIC BREECHES

Narciso

Narciso Verbicaro, the eldest child of Giuseppe and Rosari, was slow-witted. He was also, from his youth until his last breath, elegantly slender in a charcoal double-breasted coat and wide pleated trousers. A childhood spent in the egg candler's and two leather tanneries led to an adolescence hauling debris from the buildings his father demolished. Narciso would run from the rubble to the trailer all day, back and forth, his skinny arms filled with broken boards and bricks, a cigarette nearly touching the brim of his fedora, while Giuseppe swung his hammer and cursed at the things he hit. The wheelbarrow was too complicated for Narciso, all the loading and balancing and preparing a path over ditches and bumps, so he carried everything, all day, in his arms.

In those days old Moe Blumenfeld, the racetrack owner who paid the local Italians to clear his lots, liked to park his Duesenberg and watch. He'd see the old man attack a house like an ax murderer and he'd smile; he'd see the little mountains of planks and stone, propelled by the skinny legs of a boy hidden beneath the rubble, fly across the yard, and he'd laugh.

They called Narciso by the last part of his name, pronounced *cheese-o,* or they called him Lucky Pants because of the Italian folktale of the magic breeches which filled with an endless supply of gold coins. Narciso had deep pockets filled with keys and pocket knives and lighters and candy and, later in life, money. He always seemed to have whatever was needed right there in his pants. The family thought an angel or the devil himself followed him around, filled his pockets, yanked his collar a second before a truck might squish him. To them he seemed a man living in a dream, charmed and free of worries, but asleep at the wheel.

In fact, behind the wheel was his favorite place. Narciso learned to drive his father's Model T when he was twelve because Giuseppe had no patience for a machine and beat it with his hands and feet whenever it confounded him. By contrast, Narciso was as gentle with a machine as he was with dogs and mules and nanny goats; he coaxed the Tin Lizzy into gear, talked it around sharp turns with a loaded trailer in back, sang it through busy intersections. He was a hazard, to be sure, because his mind was a tabula rasa, and he drove as if on an empty road while others screeched and swerved around him. He laid the windshield down and set the looking glass so he could watch himself drive, watch his hair sweep back with the wind and see his handsome face beam in the shadow breaks of passing trees and buildings and trucks, his young life there before him, filled with adventure and beauty and charm.

Women adored him. Powerful men confided in him. He gave money away, once a twenty to a bootlegger at a speakeasy because the man had just lost his shirt at poker and Ciso had just gotten paid.

Two weeks later the racketeer gave Narciso a shiny black Packard. The young man took friends and family on thrilling rides about town until Giuseppe returned from two months working north of the bay. The old man promptly hitched his yard trailer to the beautiful sedan and had his son drive it to his next demolition job.

By the mid-1940s Narciso and his younger brothers had found their way to the other side of their father's coin, pouring foundations and filling East Bay swamp with apartments during the war boom years. By the end of Eisenhower and the first year of the Catholic presidency, Narciso met daily with his brothers and their friends for breakfast at a Holiday Inn near the freeway, ostensibly to be in on the schemes and deals they discussed. Then he would wander in his convertible Cadillac, play golf, pick up groceries for his wife or mother, visit a building site, or yak with some guys leaning on shovels. He often drove his wife, Alice Elaine, to stores and forgot her, taking off alone while she was shopping or in the ladies' room. She would call for a ride, sometimes to Narciso's brother Ludovico. Lu, she would shout into the pay phone's mouthpiece, Ciso took off again. Is he at the office? Ludovico would leave his desk, cursing, and give Alice and her groceries a ride home.

One lovely afternoon in the Kennedy years Narciso took Alice Elaine to the Hink's department store in Berkeley and left her there while she was trying on pedal pushers. He headed north from the San Francisco Bay on Interstate 80, absorbed in a radio program about Mel Tormé, and by the time he reached the Sierras he was hungry and wondering if he shouldn't try to get home before dark. He took an exit, unable to read the sign (he'd never actually learned to read), and found a restaurant with a gold mining motif, with old picks and pans and shovels hanging on the walls.

Ciso was fifty-three, but he looked as if the numbers were reversed to the waitress who kept laughing and squeezing his pin-striped arm and leg. She wanted to know if he had seen that funny colored guy in Reno, Sammy Davis? Ciso offered to drive the waitress there, and soon they were at Donner Pass, winding down the old highway in the dark with the top up because the snow was dancing across the road, Ciso taking the hairpin turns fast enough to make the Caddy's fins tap the guard rails at the edges of thousand-foot cliffs. By the time they reached Truckee the young woman begged to be let out of the car, her face white as the snow on the peaks around them. Ciso got coffee, consulted the compass next to the Virgin on his dashboard (both desperate gifts from his wife), and took off alone, thinking he was heading toward home.

Frank Sinatra owned the Cal-Neva Casino on the north shore of Lake Tahoe, and this was where Narciso's Cadillac found itself late that evening, under a clear and frigid sky. The mountain air and the sweet scent of ponderosa pine needles filled his nostrils. He didn't mind being lost. Wherever he ended up always seemed an opportunity for some adventure, some flirtation or conversation, something new to see. Ciso's mind was pre-Copernican: the sun and its planets, the galaxies and constellations, which he thought of as lanterns hanging from a ceiling, orbited the fixed place where he stood. In his geocentric cosmos, mysteries, such as why those candles were snuffed every morning, didn't bother him. High in the Sierras, in Old Blue Eyes' parking lot, he could see thousands of them flickering in the heavens, lighting his way to the craps tables.

It often infuriated Ludovico and the other siblings that Lucky Pants didn't much care for gambling. He loved casinos, but he rarely played. His brothers and sisters, his sons and nieces and nephews, would lose their shirts and curse. They'd beg him to play and, after an hour or so, he might saunter up to the wheel of fortune, lay a few fivers on a twenty, and win a hundred dollars. Then he'd lend them the hundred to play with, and watch.

That night Johnny Rosselli, who'd torpedoed for Capone in Chicago and snuffed more victims in LA for Jack Dragna, and who was rubbing elbows those days with Sinatra, the Kennedy brothers, and Ronald Reagan, waved him over. Aren't you a friend of Joe Bonanno's in Frisco? Johnny asked.

Narciso remembered Joe from the old neighborhood all right. Sure. Played boccie with his pop, Giuseppe. The muscle at the table made room, a half-dozen guys without necks, and Rosselli had Narciso's ear for an hour while the slow-witted dandy nodded and laughed in all the right places. Drinks, pig's knuckles, pasta, and calamari, all on the house, were brought to Narciso as he listened to Johnny talk about Hollywood and politics. These fucking politicians, Rosselli said, his boozy breath spraying Narciso's nose, are the biggest whores of all. Worse than any girls we pimped in Long Beach.

Johnny, I don't know nothin' about politics. I don't even want to know nothin'.

Hey! Rosselli slapped his back. You're smart. The old murderer staggered to his feet. You're smart. He waved a finger, and he and his entourage made their way to some privileged room beyond the lounge.

Some time later a guy with a big Adam's apple was beside Narciso in the gents'. He wore a Hawaiian shirt and the kind of checked slacks popular that year on golf courses, iridescent green and orange. Excuse me. I wonder could you give me some advice, the guy said. Narciso nodded and shook himself at the urinal. You see, I fried my engine coming over the mountains, and I can't get a cab up here in the boondocks, and all's I need is to go a few miles to this Travelodge.

You need a ride? Narciso asked.

Oh, man, that would be fantastic! I got a woman waitin' for me in this motel, if you know what I mean. He chuckled, and Ciso joined in. Matter of fact I got two women there, couple of showgirls. Can't keep the girls waiting, can we? Name's Charlie Fusetti. I sell cars in Omaha. He offered his hand.

Narciso Verbicaro, Charlie.

Charlie, whose real name was Mark Hendley, and whose former occupation was special agent for the CIA, on temporary suspension, directed Narciso to follow the lakeshore into Nevada. Hendley had been suspended for using excessive force, and he had a reputation for the same dating back to his years as a soldier of fortune in Latin America, where he and a partner had committed murder and various acts of torture on banana farmers. He was hoping to take the driver to a motel room which he and the same partner had filled with divers instruments of persuasion in order to find out what was in the cigar box Johnny Rosselli had given Narciso, figuring this would put him back in good order with the department, but somewhere in the middle of Hendley's phony patter about car sales Narciso had made a turn from the lakeshore highway. An hour later they were winding through the mountains, among the flocked pines, and Hendley was giggling nervously.

You know your way around these woods, Ciso?

Jesus, these trees just get prettier the higher we go, don't they, Charlie? His tires hit a patch of snow and fishtailed.

Think we should maybe turn around? He reached under his garish shirt to touch his .38 revolver.

Let's try this. Ciso turned right where the road forked, and the Caddy started winding down the eastern slope. The pines gave way, slowly, to sagebrush.

Are we lost, Ciso? He laughed. I'm lost, I'll tell you that!

Ciso said nothing for a minute, and Hendley's mind raced with images of desert burial, of his head and hands severed and fed to coyotes while the rest of him was spaded under a creosote bush. I think we're okay, Ciso said. There's always some little jerkwater town in places like this.

Sure enough, a bullet-blasted sign with the name *Genoa* appeared in the headlights, just as Ciso's Caddy took its last gulps of gas. The nationality of the town's name didn't help Mark Hendley's stomach. He sat on the edge of the seat as Ciso threw the car into neutral and coasted the last couple of miles to the general store and filling station, as if by some practiced routine. The building was

dark. Ciso tapped the horn. Hendley gripped the handle of his revolver.

A geezer in overalls staggered out of the building. Closed! he
yelled.

Fill her up? Ciso waved a twenty out the window. Hendley slid
out of the shotgun seat, saying he'd better call the girls at the motel.
Good idea, Ciso said. The agent called his partner and tried to describe where he and the suspect were.

Didn't you hear me? The geezer spat and walked up to Ciso's
window. The till is closed. I can't make no change. Ciso told him to
keep the change.

A couple of hours later the sun was peeking over a range of
barren mountains to the east, and the sage desert stretched in all directions around them. They had already passed a DANGER, DO NOT
ENTER, ATOMIC TESTING SITE sign, and Hendley had convinced Narciso to turn around. Now the top was down, the frigid air was rich
with the scent of sage, the radio was playing show tunes from LA,
and Hendley had given up on his partner. He was wondering if he
shouldn't just waste the old greaseball out here in the middle of
nowhere and boost his car. Narciso opened the cigar box and offered Hendley a foot-long Cuban Corona.

They were doing ninety on a pencil-straight highway which
ended in a mountain range, perhaps twenty miles distant, perhaps
fifty. To the north was a tiny dust cloud moving slowly toward the
highway. Hendley held the cigar and laughed. Cigars, he said.

The best, Charlie. Ciso reached into his pants and produced a

Zippo. The dust cloud got larger over time and grew wheels and vague geometric proportions. It was approaching the highway slowly, on a perpendicular trajectory. These are the very best, Charlie. We gotta enjoy life, right?

Hendley cupped his hands around the flame, drew on the cigar, leaned back in his seat, and laughed. He laughed with great embarrassment and relief, in great clouds of smoke. Narciso steered with his knees and lit a stogie for himself, laughing along. The vehicle running on a perpendicular track was identifiable now, an ancient flatbed truck, its cargo a flock of dusty sheep, its driver a small fellow in a slouched cowboy hat, bouncing up and down, staring straight ahead. Hendley watched him approach through clouds of cigar smoke, through gasps of laughter. The cowboy never moved his head to right or left, and Narciso never relented on the gas pedal. It didn't seem possible to the suspended special agent, with a thousand square miles around them, with only two vehicles on that planar expanse of the planet, with the truck creeping along a separate road and Ciso flying across the blacktop to the horns of Jimmy Lunceford's Swing Band, that there could be a collision, and so his last thoughts were happy ones.

The truck crept across the highway, and Ciso hit it. Former Agent Hendley flew through the windshield and was killed instantly, as were three sheep. The man in the front of the truck fell drunkenly onto the desert and cursed the bumps and bruises he received. The Cadillac was destroyed, squashed like a grape under an immense foot. Narciso was thrown into the air.

He hung there for some time, a hundred miles from an atom-bomb crater, a hundred yards from a billboard with the legs of chorus girls and the words *Last Chance* painted across it. He floated above the frost-rimed sagebrush, the branches aflame with sunrise, and fell to earth among the crying lambs, unhurt, cushioned by the beautiful fleece and the soft flesh of God's innocent creatures.

THE DIVINE COMEDY

Angelo

ecause his mother and the allergist thought he should avoid breathing, because his father rarely took notice, and because he fell dead center in a clan of athletic or adorable siblings, Angelo Verbicaro started making weird noises, squeaky voices slid through the cracks of doors, impersonations of family who'd just stepped off the boat.

His brother, Paulie, and sister Penny fled when they heard him coming. He was a pest, a raspy adenoidal racket that followed them to the bathroom door. The younger ones, however, wet their diapers for a bark or a Bronx cheer, and his mother, a sad, dour woman with a beautiful face, choked on her Parliaments when he did a line from *Caesar,* when he stormed like Gleason. He realized that the more embarrassing and heartbreaking the material, the bigger were his mother's coughing fits and his classmates' groans. Bathroom humor, embarrassing noises attributed to himself and his obese or nervous teachers, the voices and gestures of his cousins from the old country, were part of a repertoire which always featured himself as the most pathetic creature in the script, the recipient of fortune's cruelest tricks. In Angie's shtick he made himself the weakling who got smacked in the chops or fooled by idiots.

Imitation was his currency. He lacked the physical grace of his older siblings, the sweetness of his younger siblings, the mathematical mind and tenacity of his father, the compassion of his mother and aunts, the strength and optimism of his extended family. To Angie, most of life seemed a hoax, and somehow it helped to imitate it, helped to pay attention to the serious way people said and did things.

His father, Joe, wasn't a big man, but he rocked on the balls of his feet and looked people dead in the eye, ever poised to take on the world. He had an easy stride and a big grin for strangers, a ruggedly handsome face punctuated by a broken nose and skin darker than that of a black man who occasionally caddied for him on the golf course. One Saturday Joe dragged Angelo out of bed to caddy with his brother and cousins Gino and Mario. Joe's leather bag hung easily from Paulie's broad shoulders like a quiver of arrows and made him look a bit like Robin Hood in his green baseball cap. Gino and Mario, two muscular guys with rolled-up sleeves, carried their clubs like notebooks. Somehow Angie, who had inherited the worst of both grandfathers, the Irish maternal one's slight frame with the Italian paternal one's huge schnoz and lack of grace, was given the biggest bag, Uncle Narciso's ostentatious spumoni-colored Cadillac with the baroque bangles and the many pockets filled with balls, tees, and bottles of Scotch.

Joe was a serious golfer, and Uncle Ludovico was serious to the point of a heart attack on the greens, but Uncle Narciso was always out in the rough without a care in his heart. He had an elaborate ritual to perform before each shot. He'd stretch his arms, roll his head on his shoulders, then shake his butt like a rumba dancer, rattling the change and keys and nail clippers in his baggy trousers before slowly cocking his arms. His swing was wild, and he occasionally hit the ball squarely, but usually he sliced it into another fairway or chased snakes thirty yards away, and as often as not he swung and missed altogether. *Steeeerike one!* Angie growled. Ciso laughed, and Lu fumed.

Long drive down the third base line, right between Davenport's legs! Angie's voice, behind his cupped hands, had the timbre of Russ Hodges's on a transistor radio speaker. *It'll stay fair if it doesn't hit that catalpa tree!*

Ciso's ball hit the tree and bounced onto the fairway, then rolled another fifty yards down the asphalt caddy-cart trail. Joe laughed. Lucky Pants strikes again, he said.

Angie followed his uncle with the enormous bag, off the fairway, into the eucalyptus trees and the gopher dirt. His little alien voices and radio commentary didn't faze Ciso a bit, even as balls ricocheted off trees and landed at their feet. Oops, Ciso would say. That was a close one.

On the green Uncle Lu raged and beat the ground with his putter. Joe was killing them, but what killed Lu most was that Ciso, after twelve strokes out in the forest, would sink a putt from thirty yards right after Lu had missed a five-footer. Son of a goddamned blue baboon's ass! Lu yelled. He snapped his putter in half over his knee and tossed it into a briar patch.

Hey, Lu, Ciso called.

What the hell do you want? Lu paced around the next tee.

Lu, this boy's a natural. He's like that goddamn guy in Reno. What the hell's his name?

Ciso, don't talk to me right now. While Lu paced, Joe grinned and elbowed Ciso. The boys grinned as well, but Lu's sons knew better than to laugh aloud. Joe crooned like Sinatra and teed his ball. One of those bells that now and then rings, Joe sang. Just one of those things.

We gotta take this boy to Reno, Ciso said. Joe, Joe, Joe. He's a natural. He's like that goddamned guy at Harrah's.

You can't take a kid to the casino, Joe said. It's against the law. He smacked the ball beautifully, a straight, lofty drive that disappeared a moment in the blade glitter of the eucalyptus beyond the green and then reappeared on the fairway, and as Angie watched it and heard the clapping and hoots of approval he saw himself under the flickering marquee lights of Reno. His lips, an inch from the head of a nine iron, mouthed the words: *Thank you, ladies and gentlemen. I love you, you're beautiful. Thank you, thank you, thank you.*

Two weeks later Angie climbed from the temperate bay and the steamy valley over the granite spine of California, then dropped to the Nevada desert. His ears and sinuses popped and shrank until it seemed the geography of his face might change as much as the terrain out the window. He listened to the guys talk about gambling strategies, Lu and Bobby Rich, the highway patrolman, in the front seat of Ciso's Cadillac, with Ciso adding his two bits from the back with Angie. He watched the desert surround them like a wilderness of certain death. He rubbed his sweaty palms together.

It was Ciso's cockamamy idea to let his nephew join their routine junket. The guys drove up here twice a month on a Friday morning and came back sometime Saturday or Sunday. They always took Ciso's car and never let Ciso drive it. Their wives gave them a set amount to lose or win, and every few months the ladies came, too, and insisted on motel rooms. Rich, the cop, always lost everything, got drunk, and begged money off Ciso, who always gave him some. Lu would come out ahead about one time in five, just enough to make him agonize over every card or number. Ciso would watch the shows, flirt and talk, and occasionally play and win or lose. He'd get corralled by real estate schemers, religious fanatics, and transparent con men with dead eyes. He'd run into mobsters whose fathers knew him from the old neighborhood in San Francisco. He'd laugh and nod to everybody.

Ciso's plan was to let Angie hang out in the restaurant with him and, after a while, sneak into the gaming area at his side. They'd spent a half hour drinking coffee and Cokes before Angie watched the ugliest man he'd ever seen shamble up and shake hands with his uncle. This swarthy monster, a man with huge lumps on his face and pointed yellow teeth, talked about horses with Ciso, then motioned for him and Angie to follow him to the slots.

Ciso gave his nephew a stack of nickels to drop into a slot machine while he talked with the behemoth, a guy Uncle Lu later referred to as Jimmy the Finger. Angie won a dollar on a nickel. The machine flashed and jangled as the coins spilled into its receptacle. The two men laughed and slapped his back.

It was a few years after Sputnik, which had happened the same week Angie's grandfather had dropped dead in San Francisco. He always connected the two events in his mind, the old womanizing Italian patriarch keeling over on the beach and this tiny Russian spirit beeping in the heavens, circling dangerously about the earth. It was the year before Nikita Khrushchev got the notion to slip some missiles under Jack Kennedy's nose. It was a night that changed Angie's life.

It had something to do with the wrinkly necks and the old-goat tobacco and Brylcreem smells of his uncles while they stood in that crowd of people waiting for the floor show. After his long day of travel and gambling nickels and walking down the streets of the desert town to snoop in pawnshops and field questions from winos and con men, he imagined he would look and smell like his uncles someday, that he would shuffle into the darkness with other souls, all of them waiting for something which they couldn't understand and were anxious to see. The gates to the show were guarded by Jimmy the Finger and two other monsters, and the people who descended stepped uncertainly like frightened children, their drinks held aloft like lanterns and their small miseries plain on their faces. Angie felt almost invisible among these people in the middle of their lives, people feeling their way down a dark path; he felt un-

formed while they were shaped and sculpted grotesquely by the be-
liefs and fears of a lifetime, wrinkled by worries and greed and
cheating, swollen by depression and gluttony and lust. When the
monster with yellow fangs touched his shoulder and parted the aisle
to lead their foursome to a front-row table, the stage lights glowed
before him like embers. Angie breathed deeply.

Rich stifled sobs and wiped his florid face. Angie's uncles patted the patrolman's shoulders and offered cheerful words, but the
old cop said he was a worthless piece of shit who drank and gam-
bled and didn't deserve his lovely wife. He needed to tell all of them
that he had been a good man once, a decorated soldier and steady
husband and father, before he'd become a worthless piece of shit.
Chorus girls and a singer in sailor blues did a couple of numbers,
the women's legs and breasts swinging hypnotically before Angie's
face as the old cop snuffled. Then the main act walked on stage.

A man known as a lovable cherub with a speech disorder in
movies and TV became a foul-mouthed, crotch-snatching, mean-
spirited wise guy on stage. Rich's blubbery face blended with the
embarrassed, laughing ones around him, and Angie sat, stunned. It
was beautiful and horrible to watch the performer and his audience.
The man spoke of hemorrhoids, and the people squirmed in their
seats. He spoke of cruelty and infidelity, of alcoholics and immigrants with thick accents, while people keeled over. A spotlight
swept the casino and came to rest on Angie. You, the comedian said.
Come up here.

He froze until Ciso and Lu nudged and practically lifted him on stage. Then he stood on some ledge above the contorted faces in brilliant light, afraid to move. When the mike swung under his face, Angie asked, What do you want?

What do I want? People laughed, and the comedian waited. Angie's knees shook, his heart pounded in his throat. What do I want? Well, I don't want any shit from you, kid! What's your name?

Why?

Why? The casino shook with laughter. This goddamned kid don't trust me! Hey, I'll tell you what I want: Why weren't you laughing at my shtick?

I thought I was. I'm sorry.

HEY! DON'T PITY ME, KID! Angie could see the beads of sweat shake off the comedian's face, the slick makeup. You ain't perfect yourself! I noticed you got a few zits on your face, Kid!

Angie waited for the noise to die down. He caught his breath. Actually, sir, I got a whole mountain range of zits.

Mountain range? Like the Sierra Nevada? You got ski resorts, too?

I don't think so, sir. I mean, don't you need snow?

The comedian waited for the laughing to stop and eyed Angie with the same aggression he'd seen in the eyes of Jimmy the Finger when he'd tossed a drunk out the door. Then he put his arm on the boy's shoulder and looked around. It was a hammy, conspiratorial gesture. When I was your age, he said, they told me that the only way to get rid of my zits was to go get schtooked.

Angie waited a long time. His heart was pounding so hard he thought he would keel over, but a voice was coming to him. The voice he found was an adolescent version of the man's beside him: *And where does a guy get schtooked, if you don't mind my asking?*

Again the comedian had to wait. Something between a smile and a grimace crossed his features. *I'll tell you what not to do, kid. Don't go into a drugstore, like I did, and ask, Can I get schtooked here?*

Angie could hear moans and barks of laughter. The comedian's thick hand was still on his shoulder, damp and warm as a facecloth. Angie cleared his throat. *You mean the pharmacist wouldn't let you get schtooked?*

NOT EVEN FOR SIX BITS, KID! NOT EVEN BACK THERE NEXT TO THE GERITOL AND THE PREPARATION H!

Jeez. Angie shook his head. He could see Uncle Lu's teeth gleaming red with the lights and Rich's contorted face leaning against Ciso's shoulder. *Well, since you ain't got zits no more, you musta got schtooked somewheres.*

Kid. The comedian shook his head, patted Angie's shoulder, and looked around the theater. *Kid, I got schtooked so many places and in so many ways, if I told you half of them they'd kick me outta this place. They'd toss me in the middle of Lake Tahoe.*

Wow. Angie stood with his mouth open a moment, gazing into the spotlights, while the crowd roared and convulsed. A woman with sciatica bent double and had to be carried out at the end of the show. An obese Realtor choked on a wad of Bazooka Bubble Gum. *Must be one of them product advertisement restrictions or something.*

You might could say that, kid.

I never even seen one ad for getting schtooked, though.

The comedian started to speak, but an amazing thing happened: his mouth widened into a laugh! People were crying, blowing their noses, falling and writhing on the floor while the comedian laughed and Angie stared in wonder at the lights. Years from then he would remember the lights and the man's hand on his shoulder, damp and warm through his acrylic dress shirt. When his brother would return from Vietnam crazy and addicted to heroin, when his father would take him to see Bobby Rich's yellowish body in the casket; when his older sister would disappear with the criminal she fell in love with, he'd return to that evening onstage beside the comedian.

Kid, you'd be surprised. *Ahem!* The man was having trouble speaking, his hand was twitching, and all Angie had to do was stand there with his look of innocence, with his all-American gaze of ignorance and awe. Kid. If I'm not mistaken, there's some ladies, *ahem!* There's some ladies right in this casino who advertise for getting schtooked, but don't quote me on this.

Certain advertising restrictions must apply, Angie said.

Exactly. And let me give you some . . . The man's voice trailed off, and his eyes squeezed shut. His entire pudgy body shook in the stiff tuxedo. People were coughing, choking, dropping out of their seats. An incontinent army colonel fell to one knee and wet his trousers before he could reach the boys' room. A Catholic priest seated beside his mistress had a heart fibrillation and thought he might die. Kid, the man started to say.

He would return to that evening. Whenever he'd read about

people gassed or shot and dropped into the trenches they'd just dug, whenever he'd walk past the dying drunks and junkies on city side- walks, he'd remember that night above the crowd. He'd remember the man beside him, the grotesque faces, the agonized bodies be- neath them, and a small voice. It said, *Not you, kid. Not you.*

A TERRIBLE NEW LIFE

Paulie

A keenness left Paulie Verbicaro that summer. The oak leaves lost their teethed edges, and a ball slapped the catcher's mitt before he saw it. He drifted into the watery light of distant blue gum trees and the sudden nebula bursts of passing windshields, not knowing, for some weeks, why the world had changed, why he had fallen from grace.

Put simply, his eyes were getting weak. But the loss had been gradual, and he only sensed that he was losing his game for some bizarre reason—timing, coordination, God's idea of justice, who knows? It was Uncle Ludovico who first noticed it was vision, while they were heading to give an estimate for a driveway. Hey, you drove right past it, he said. I told you 2525, on the mailbox.

It was on the mailbox?

Yes. You blind?

No.

Lu had played third with the best, before Paulie was born, in old Seals Stadium on 16th and Bryant. In fact, he and Paulie's father, Joe, had shared the sandlots and fields of San Francisco with future stars, playing on Boys' Club teams sponsored by olive oil and produce companies. They'd chased line drives hit by the Italian pantheon which Paulie's father and all the older men spoke of in hushed tones. Frank Crosetti, who moved like a cat to snatch the ball an inch above the ground. Tony Lazzeri with his big bat and shrewd smile. The shrimp Billy Martin of the Oakland Oaks, who played like a Tasmanian devil in his private fury. On fields more gold with dandelions than green they'd played pepper with any of the DiMaggio brothers who could escape their father's fishing boat long enough to get on a diamond, Mike, Tom, Vince, Dominick, a family of prodigious hitters, three making it to the majors. In the same old wooden ballpark, under the Hamm's smokestack and against Potrero Hill, where Paulie and his father had seen the Giants play their first two seasons, Uncle Lu had swung a bat for the Missions and popped a Texas leaguer to the greatest of them all, Joe DiMaggio.

Can you read the numbers on that house?

What numbers?

Christ, no wonder you're hitting like that Who's Who Alou kid on the Giants. You need specs, like your old man.

A week into the school year he got them, big black frames like Buddy Holly's, but he left them in his glove box and only put them on to drive or to watch TV. His season was over, and he wondered if he could recover his game come spring with new eyes. Now and then he tripped on a step walking from the TV to the fridge. His feet seemed three yards from his head.

His French teacher, Mrs. Rinaldi, noticed the problem one day when she was at the board. She asked him to stay after class for a few minutes. You're off on a bad road, she said. Right now your grades are in the dustbin.

The dustbin?

And my husband says you want to play for some hotsy-totsy university.

I hope.

Which mightn't consider you if you fail this class. She sat sideways in a student desk, facing him. Her long, crossed leg swung, and Paulie could see a bit of her thigh and the lace of her slip. Can you see?

Beg pardon?

You misspelled all those verbs I conjugated on the board the other day.

I've always had a conjugal problem.

When she laughed he could see her teeth, which were a little crooked and coffee-stained. At this distance he could see the fine wrinkles around her squinched eyes, the flecks of blond in her red hair, the filigree hem of her slip. Join the club, she said.

That year, the year DiMaggio's former wife and the president's gorgeous mistress took an overdose, the Giants were the best team in baseball. They made Paulie miserable and ecstatic at the same time. Here it was September 23 and they were four games behind Los Angeles with seven left to play. Here they had gone out of their way to lose ground in the stretch, and Lu and Joe and all the older men had written them off, but Paulie had to believe in them.

He sensed that his baseball fanaticism made him weird for his age, that he lacked friends for ample reason, even though he was a nice-looking kid and a good athlete. Paulie had to listen to every game for the rest of the season and perform rituals for certain players, Mays, McCovey, Cepeda, the three Alou brothers, José Pagan, new heroes who'd come to the city of Italian gods like beautiful black and Caribbean Argonauts. He had to squeeze the visor of his cap once and touch his left foot with his right twice before they batted. He had to say the words, *Hum, baby,* in hushed tones and tap his glove with a fist between pitches.

Like DiMaggio, Paulie was tall for an Italian American, and he had a big, level swing which his father always compared to that of the great man. In addition, he was quiet and shy like Joe D., and his game was one which beat you with its beauty and not, as in the case of his father and uncle, with its dogged tenacity. Paulie loved the game and thought it the most blessed and democratic vocation in the world. He loved Orlando Cepeda, he loved the way black guys, or guys who couldn't speak English, were spoken of like family members at the dinner table. He loved the way little guys and fat guys who would be trampled or laughed at on a gridiron or basketball court could win by their craft and idiosyncrasies, by fashioning a knuckler or a perfect swing, like some artisan at his bench, and bringing it to bear in the clutch.

Baseball touched the deepest place in Paulie. He pictured one spring day in an African valley when some knuckle-draggers learned to feed their young by throwing cobbles at an ibis or swinging branches at hyenas. Baseball felt like what his body was meant to do. The way ballplayers moved embodied some mythic system of personality. The way first basemen and catchers and shortstops and relief pitchers moved was as distinct from their fellows as figures along nine stations in a zodiac.

And the Giants had it all, but they also had the single greatest player in the game, a man whose presence shone above the others like Achilles driving his chariot before the walls of Troy: Willie Mays. Even so, the Dodgers usually found their weak heel and beat them with pitching and cunning, and now they were ahead by four with seven left, and only a fool would hope as he hoped. He ducked out of school at lunchtime in order to park by the bay and perform his hat and foot rituals while listening to the game against Houston. It worked: the Giants won, and Los Angeles lost to Saint Louis.

On Tuesday neither team played, and Paulie sat in class thinking: Three down with six to play. He didn't hear Mrs. Rinaldi's question until she'd repeated it: *Ou est la bibliotheque? Monsieur Paul, attention, s'il vous plait.*

She kept him after class again and had him practice conjugating verbs. She made him scoot a desk right up to the board where she wrote the verbs, and when her back was to him he watched the way her dress moved over her hips as she wrote. She turned and leaned over him and had him watch her lips as she enunciated. When he pursed his lips and copied what her mouth did she congratulated him. So, why did you miss class yesterday?

I got sick. Something I ate in the cafeteria.

The next day, Wednesday, he skipped class again and listened on the transistor radio as the Giants beat the Cardinals. Russ Hodges, the Giants' announcer, kept him updated on the Dodgers' loss to the Houston Colt Forty-fives. Paulie danced along the bay, on a strip of scummy sand and sea cobbles near the freeway. A couple of old Japanese men with bamboo fishing rods asked about the scores. They smacked his shoulders, and one of the guys gave Paulie a bottle of beer with an unreadable label. Two down with five to go!

Mrs. Rinaldi saw him in the hall before lunch Thursday and warned him about the trouble he'd be in if he skipped class. The veins in her neck stood out, and she looked older than he remembered. One day of three is a poor average, she said. He tried to guess her age that afternoon, assessing the various parts of her body, her long legs, the loose skin of her upper arms, the nest of wrinkles around her nervous eyes, the flecks of blond or silver in her auburn hair. Neither French nor Italian, Mrs. Rinaldi was a British girl who'd married an American GI during the war, one of his uncle's golf cronies, a little old man who drank whiskey on the course and sold houses up and down the East Bay. Paulie knew she wasn't near as old as Pete Rinaldi. That day when he left her class he meandered home in his jalopy, listening to the end of the game as he circled Lake Merrit in Oakland. His team won without his help, but so did the Dodgers. Two down, four to go.

Friday there was a verb quiz, and Paulie thought he did okay. Mrs. Rinaldi looked frayed around the edges when she handed out the mimeographed sheets, as if she hadn't slept well. Even her dress was kind of lumpy-looking, thick and unpressed. She yelled at two girls for what Paulie thought was no reason. He left class in time to hear the Giants lose, and he blamed himself for not keeping the fires burning.

On Saturday San Francisco split a double-header with Houston, and Paulie's dad said, That's all she wrote. That night the boy cruised in his salt-faded Ford sedan. He drove it slowly up and down the avenue in a myopic daze, waving blindly to passersby. A couple of freshmen he barely knew tapped on the window at a corner, one of them brandishing a quart bottle, and Paulie threw the door open before he recognized them. The boys looked in some transitional stage between hoods and surfers, their hair slicked back, their shirts baggy madras with cigarette packs bulging in the pockets. They urged Paulie to hit his horn when some girls drove by in a '56 Chevy, and asked who he was going with, but Paulie just shrugged.

It wasn't just his vision, his entire connection to everything had lost its edge. A Saturday night, some brew, some chicks rolling by in their daddies' new cars, some guys trying to get a conversation going. Didn't register. He dropped them at a drive-in and started for home, slipping the glasses on once he'd left the main drag. At a busy intersection he saw a woman on a bus going the other way, a face ghost-doubled by her reflection in the window and half obscured by the strawberry hair falling across her cheek, and for a moment he thought it was his French teacher and slipped his glasses off.

Sunday morning he consulted the paper and was amazed to see that the Giants were down by one with one left to play. How could LA keep losing? He skipped church and took the rooter bus from Richmond to Candlestick among a crowd of old people in dark glasses and hooded sweatshirts, or black windbreakers and baseball caps, near-identical men and women who passed a hat and dropped nickels on total runs, score spreads, number of home runs, number of hits, number of beanballs, maybe number of rhubarbs, who knows, all entrusted to a wiry old lady with a clipboard and coin pouch in her purse. Paulie was the only kid, and he ran to the ticket booths and managed to get into the bleachers in time to watch batting practice. McCovey slammed one off a girder supporting the scoreboard, and it ricocheted twenty feet above Paulie's head. The voice on the PA said it was fan appreciation day, and that five people with lucky seat numbers could win a car, but this didn't include bleacher seats.

The game progressed slowly, punctuated by blasts of maritime wind and islands of sunshine. A subtle raking slant to the light and smoky taste to the air told him that fall was truly here and ball play soon a memory. Southpaw Billy O'Dell threw for San Francisco, and not much happened at the plate for either team until Ed Bailey, a squat catcher who looked like a balding mechanic, cracked a homer near Paulie's seat, and then, a couple of innings later, Houston hit Billy three times and tied the score, one each. By then Los Angeles had begun playing St. Louis, and the scoreboard that loomed above Paulie at an oblique angle showed the series of zeroes as the innings passed four hundred miles south.

In the bottom of the eighth Willie Mays dug his foot into the dirt and double-cocked his bat. Paulie squeezed his visor and tapped his feet together. The organist squeaked the first bar of Bye, Bye, Baby, and Mays watched the first ball go by for a strike. The song stopped, the crowd fell silent. Mays was zero for his last ten at bats. Paulie whispered, *Hum, baby,* twice. He added a Lord's Prayer. Willie crucified the next pitch, and the Giants coasted to a win.

Few people left the stadium, however. Paulie and the others

swiveled their upper bodies as if receiving yoga instructions en masse. The scoreboard looming over his left shoulder showed seven zeroes for Saint Louis, six for Los Angeles. In a moment another square zero appeared, and several people clapped.

Paulie dug out the transistor and stuck its nipple in his ear. Russ Hodges blabbered about the car drawing, and Paulie saw a convertible roll out onto the field, as if part of a beauty pageant. A couple of middle-aged guys with New York accents moved into a gap beside him and asked what was what on the radio. One let his hairy forearm lie against Paulie's knee the way he might with a buddy in a dugout. Who's up for St. Louie?

Paulie explained that Hodges was getting updates from Vince Scully in LA, but it was kind of periodic. Still scoreless in the top of the eighth. Wait. Fly to left field, caught by Davis. One out.

Jesus, the guy next to him said, does this bring back memories? He started to describe a story Paulie knew well, about the pennant playoff in which Bobby Thompson hit his home run, and though it was a familiar tale of his father's and uncle's Paulie hung on every word because this guy had lived in Queens when it happened and could describe the sensation in the streets. His mind felt split in two, with one ear listening to Hodges give the count in LA alongside his patter about Folger's Coffee while the other ear took in the Polo Grounds and a street in New York in 1951.

An attractive woman stepped onto the field to claim her car, and the crowd cheered. Although her hair was dark, there was something in her manner of walking which made Paulie think of Mrs. Rinaldi, and he pictured her pursed lips as she leaned over him after school. *Je n'ai pas ta plume, je suis dans mon lit.* I don't have your pen, I'm in bed. He wondered if she shared a bed with her wizened little husband and hoped that, like Lucy and Ricky on TV, she had her own.

Hodges was talking with Bill King about basketball when he fairly yelped, What? He did what? Just a minute, let's get that for sure . . .

Something happened, Paulie said. Several people leaned near him now. He leaped to his feet: Gene Oliver hit a homer for the Cards! The guys from New York stood next to him, and the man with the hairy arms squeezed his shoulders as they both hopped up and down, making the plank of the bleachers flex.

There were pockets of applause, scattered sections of the stadium rumbling like the first waves of an earthquake as it might ripple through the concrete structure. The woman on the field turned to wave, and Paulie thought it might be her narrow shoulders and long neck which made him think of his teacher. Then, as the deep, sonorous voice on the PA spread the news, the entire ballpark shook and roared. Some of the Giants jumped onto the field and danced around, and the woman joined in, spinning with Juan Maricial until her dress opened like a flower.

An hour later Paulie was on the rooter bus as it rocked above the downtown on its approach to the Bay Bridge. Windows of the skyscrapers were orange with the approach of evening. Half of the passengers were sauced, and the old lady with the clipboard staggered up the aisle as she handed around fistfuls of coins to the people on her list. Sirens and horns and fire bells sounded all over the city. People waved from their cars, threw cups and scraps of newspaper out their windows. The old guy beside him opened a bottle of Hamm's, and some of it misted Paulie's glasses while more of it lapped onto the man's trousers. Paulie closed his eyes as the bus entered the understory of the bridge.

ince the pennant playoff games were televised in the evenings, he didn't skip French. Mrs. Rinaldi made him sit in the front, and he could smell her perfume and chalk dust. It made an ecclesiastical mixture, a memory of limestone, rosewater, and incense. *In nomine patris, et filii, et spiritus sancti, amen. Je n'ai pas ta plume, je suis dans mon lit.*

His entire family sat before the black-and-white TV eating meatloaf and watched the Giants clobber LA eight to nothing in the first game. His brother Angie taunted the Dodgers' hitters between pitches: Hey batta, hey batta, hey batta, SWING batta!

The next evening started out the same, to the point of boring his sisters and parents, and Paulie couldn't believe how those poor bastard Dodgers were crumbling. He'd seen them beat San Francisco more often than lose to them, and usually by the craft of Sandy Koufax or Don Drysdale, who would shut them out, or little Maury Wills, who would bunt or walk or beg his way to first base, steal second, and score on either a hit-and-run, sacrifice fly, or weakly slapped base hit. None of the Dodgers seemed to know how to swing a bat, in Paulie's estimation, but they could make contact and move runners home. He heard Russ Hodges say that they were now scoreless in the last thirty-five innings! Poor luckless bastards. He went to the kitchen and fixed a salami sandwich.

The briefest tremor of pity for Los Angeles, for its millions of hapless fans, swept through him as he sliced the greasy meat. When he came back his little sisters were watching a cartoon. Paulie almost turned the channel back, but his mother told him it was their turn. It only took two games to win that rarest of baseball events, a pennant playoff, and the Giants were ahead 5-0 in the sixth inning of the second game. He finished his sandwich, got out his transistor radio, and opened his French text to an assignment due the next day.

The Dodgers had just scored seven runs.

Paulie told his father, and they commandeered the TV. He got the mitt and cap and began his rituals, but LA won it, 8–7.

One more game.

The next day American spy planes obtained photos from above the island of Cuba. The handsome young Catholic president met in secret with his military advisers, grim men with black eyebrows and silver crew cuts. A bald, gap-toothed Russian peasant and a tall Caribbean ballplayer with a bushy beard were the subject of their secret meeting. As they met, the Giants waited in a motel for evening to come to Chavez Ravine.

The shades were drawn, and the men stationed themselves before the TV. Some smoked cigars, and at least one sipped whiskey. The women and children stayed out of the living room except to make brief forays into the smoke to learn the score. Joe Verbicaro passed chips to his brother, who dropped them in front of Pete Rinaldi, the Realtor. Joe's nephew Gino picked them up and passed them to Paulie, who balanced the bowl on his mitt. Pete cleared his throat: What's the score?

Get your head out of your ass, Ludovico told him. Don't know the score.

The others laughed, including Pete. It's two-zip, Joe said. Don't listen to him, Pete.

Who's ahead?

Christ sake, he don't even know who's ahead? This is historical, *baboso*. Pay attention.

We're ahead, Paulie said. In the distorted, smoky black-and-white picture the Dodgers looked inadequate beside the Giants, they looked soft and oafish. As if the smog and heat of Los Angeles, the false dreams and sexual warmth of Disneyland and Hollywood, sapped a man's strength and left him unfocused, uncoordinated. Their fans were the same, they always had some guy with a bugle and a casual bunch of sleeveless, suntanned people yelling *Charge* and laughing right afterward, even as they were losing. Weak. Paulie tapped his glove.

Who's that? The guy warming up?

Don't tell him, Lu said. Joe. He's gotta learn to open his eyes and ears.

Hey, my wife's on it. Don't blame me, my wife won't let me watch. He winked at Joe.

No excuse, Lu said.

Tommy Davis hit a two-run homer, and the men cursed and

tossed pillows on the floor. For the next half hour the living room was quiet, save for a few whistles from Pete and curses from Lu and Joe. At the end of the eighth the Dodgers led by two.

What happens if we lose?

That's all she wrote, Joe answered.

They don't play again tomorrow?

We lose, there ain't no tomorrow, *capice?* Lu said.

Pete slopped whiskey onto his hand as he poured. That's a shame.

No shit, Joe said. Excuse my French.

Paulie closed his eyes and prayed silently. He was like a man whose girlfriend has just met a handsome millionaire who speaks five languages and drives an Aston Martin. He'd given his heart, and he wouldn't let go now.

In the top of the ninth Matty Alou led off with a single, and the men's yelling brought the entire family into the room. However, the next batter nearly hit into a double play. Lu and Joe cursed the batter and the manager, Alvin Dark.

What's the score?

Pete, shut up! Paulie's mother said. It's four to two, them, one out, last inning. Even Mickey and Janine know this.

Mickey had Down syndrome, and Janine was four years old.

He's drunk, Lu said. Why'd you invite him?

Paulie and his father exchanged looks. Gino laughed. Gino's mother, Paulie's Aunt Min, who clung to her son's arm as if she were watching a horror movie, suddenly laughed as well. They knew that Lu, not Joe, had invited Pete. Grouchy Lu was always inviting Pete, maybe just so he could complain. Joe barely knew the guy.

What thinks you make I'm drunk? Angie slurred his speech and staggered around the living room, making his mother and little sisters laugh.

McCovey came up to pinch hit, a towering man with a huge swing, and the Dodgers pitcher played cat-and-mouse with him on the edges of the plate until he walked him. The next man walked as well. This put Mays up with the bases loaded. I wouldn't want to be that chucker, Joe said. Not for a million bucks.

Pitcher always has the advantage, Lu said. Always. He was rocking on the couch like a heroin addict. Paulie was silently chanting the Lord's Prayer. Chavez Ravine was quiet.

Who's the colored up to bat?

Joe and Lu each grabbed an arm and a leg, and they carried little Pete Rinaldi out of the living room. Gino opened the sliding glass door, and the men dropped Pete in a chaise in the backyard and hurried back inside. What the hell, Pete said before Gino turned the latch.

Mays lashed the ball off the pitcher's glove, and a run scored. It was ruled a hit, and Paulie thought the pitcher was lucky to deflect it, lucky to be alive. When the family stopped whooping Paulie could hear the O'Malleys cheering next door. Orlando up next, down by one. Pete rattled the sliding door, then flopped back onto the chaise. Leave him there, Lu said to Gino. He's all right.

The Dodgers manager and catcher were on the mound. A new pitcher was called in. Paulie's younger siblings were drumming their hands on the floor, led by Angie's chant of Hey pitcha, hey pitcha, hey pitcha, and his older sister, the sophisticated college student, sat in a lotus position against his leg, pretending to meditate. It took years before Cepeda stepped up. He hit it deep to right, and the tying run scored on a tag-up. The entire family danced around the room, Paulie swinging his older sister, Penny, jitterbug style. Pete knocked on the glass and fell back into the chaise. The doorbell rang.

Paulie's sister Mickey let her in. The collar of her trench coat was raised, and her hair was hidden under a scarf. We kicked him out to the back, Lu told her, and she laughed. Paulie felt unmoored by the sight of her in his house, by the realization that his uncle knew her, had probably sat at a card table with her. He waved.

A wild pitch sent Mays to second. Paulie tried to contain his excitement. She was standing behind him while he sat with the cap and glove on like a little boy, a kid in thick glasses, maybe a little developmentally delayed like his sister Mickey. *Bonsoir,* Paul, she murmured, and he said, Hi, without turning.

Is your team winning the match?

We're tied. He wanted her to stop talking to him.

She stepped out back and lit a cigarette. Pete lay in the chaise, his mouth open.

They gave Bailey an intentional pass to load the bases. Tied game, two outs, bags full, last inning, and sober-faced Jim Davenport, the Gold Glove winner, the technician at third, stepped up. He watched the first pitch. He watched another. The third missed the corner. Son of a bitch, Lu said, he can't find the plate! Hey pitcha, Angie said, yer mudder wears army boots. The reliever for the best pitching staff in the game rocked back and threw it in the dirt, bringing in the go-ahead run.

For a moment the family was too stunned to cheer. Then Mickey yelled, Home run, and they all started laughing and whooping. Chavez Ravine was quiet as Alston brought in another pitcher. Mrs. Rinaldi sat on the edge of the chaise, smoking, while her husband slept. Her raised knees were pressed together, white in the scant light. The cigarette glowed near her frowning lips. Paulie watched her get up and stub it on the patio. On an error, San Francisco scored again before the last out. Six to four. Mrs. Rinaldi walked off into the dark.

When the Dodgers came up, their fans barely cheered. They were in shock, and their players looked the same. Wills stood at the plate looking lost, a space alien trapped on Earth under a thousand lights. Hey, batta, Angie said, yer sista's got a mustache. Junior Gilliam looked like he'd never seen a bat and couldn't decide where to hold it. Their last man, a pinch hitter, popped it to Mays. Willie caught it and threw it into the grandstands in one fluid motion before he leaped for joy.

Paulie spun with his sisters like a square dancer and stepped out to the front porch. He yelped at the harvest moon just rising over the Oakland Hills. He threw his hat and glove in the air, and the mitt landed on the roof. She stood with her arms out, maybe open for a hug, alone on the walkway, so he hugged her. He lifted her in the air, spun her around twice. She gasped and clung to his shoulders, the nape of his neck as she came down to earth, and they nearly toppled against the house. She still hung on a moment, in the darkness near the hedge, her ecclesiastical scent, her long, cool fingers moving from his nape to his scalp, her lips touching his cheek, then his mouth, a smoky, fruited taste of wine and ashes.

Every time his mind was consumed by the sensation of kissing her the Giants lost some ground against New York in the World Series. Their kissing was not so much a sin as a jinx, just as his leaving the mitt off and making a salami sandwich had been, an act which disturbed God's will or the team's momentum. He avoided her eyes in class and skipped a few more times for series games. They went seven against the Yankees, broken by a few days when the heavens dumped the worst storm in thirty years on San Francisco, turning some streets in the East Bay to knee-high creeks. They took Mickey Mantle and Whitey Ford, Yogi Berra and Roger Maris, the most winning team in the game, to the last inning when, down one to nothing with two outs, Matty Alou once again started a rally with a hit. Paulie stood before the plate glass of an appliance store in Berkeley with a group of older men, most of them winos he'd been meeting there on the days he skipped. His mitt was on one hand, transistor radio wire and thick glasses frames under his cap. The window set was always on, as was a wall of tubes deep inside where the salesmen in neckties gathered and smoked. Paulie saw himself in the glass and wondered what Mrs. Rinaldi would think of him here, cutting class and leaning shoulder to shoulder among old guys in similar caps who stank of piss. He felt her lips, remembered her smell. The next two men struck out.

The men on the sidewalk moaned, hugged their arms, cursed. Paulie had a brief insight about these men, that their hearts were big and broken easily, that they'd given their hearts to something or somebody and lost before. Willie Mays was up, and Paulie and the man next to him started praying out loud. Mays hit a double down the right field line, but Alou couldn't get past third. McCovey stepped up.

The wino beside him hugged his arm. Paulie watched Willie Mack hit the first pitch over the fence, making the men scream, but he knew it was foul. He labored to keep his thoughts pure, his mind with Willie Mack. He tapped the glove and said, *Hum, baby.* On the last pitch McCovey cracked a rifle shot into the outstretched glove of Bobby Richardson at second. A few inches south would have won the series. A small shift in the cosmos, in the Earth's rotation, in the place where ball and bat meet, and we'd have won. One hundred seventy-two games decided by three inches, or by Paulie's lust for his teacher.

It was October 16, and it was over. The Catholic president was meeting in secret again, knowing by now that the Soviets were constructing missiles on Cuba and shipping more, but the American public was still in the dark. Paulie's college prospects were over, his grades in the afternoon classes, particularly French and U.S. history, wadded-up piles of crap in a dustbin, his grace on the field a memory. And the memory of his teacher's lips on his, of her hands on the nape of his neck, was the only thing he could take solace in as he exchanged hugs with the stinking old men on the street and started for home.

He drove by her house a few evenings and always saw Pete's Cadillac cheek to jowl with her Studebaker in the driveway. In class she scowled at him, and on Friday she kept him after school, along with the two girls she was always yelling at, to copy words from the board. She leaned over his work, and her breast touched his elbow. *Oui, oui,* she said.

On Saturday he unloaded cement sacks for his father and uncles. Ludovico and Joe stood and gabbed while his brother Angie moved a broom and Paulie stacked the building materials, working up enough sweat to take off his shirt on a cool morning. Maybe he would do this work all his life, lifting and moving things, getting covered with dust and mud. His glasses fogged when he stopped to rest. His brother was imitating Elvis, pretending to strum the broom like a guitar, singing into it as if it were a mike on a stand. His father and uncle were arguing about the last game, Lu whining about an umpire's call while Joe spoke with calm authority.

Hell, no, Joe said, don't blame the ump. If that manager had known his ass from a hot stone, we'd have won it. If he'd put his fastest man on first to pinch run for Alou.

Alou's fast.

You're not going to tell me we can't get somebody to second base, by bunt or steal or hit-and-run, with no outs, to prepare for your big guns like Mays and McCovey? Cepeda on deck? Hell, Lu, Mays gets up with two down, and the runner should have been on second already. And when he hit that double, that runner should

have been on his bicycle with a twelve-foot lead and a three-foot
rocket up his ass. What the hell does Mays have to do to win a game
for Al Dark? Walk on goddamned water?

He practically does, for Christ sake, Lu said.

Best in the game, Joe said, and that manager can't figure out
how to use him. He looked over to Paulie and said, How's the working man? He didn't seem to notice Angie singing I Got Stung.

Paulie wiped his face with his shirt. How does Mays compare
with DiMaggio?

I didn't say he was DiMaggio, Joe said.

Nobody plays like DiMaggio, Lu said. They'd had this conversation before.

On Tuesday evening Paulie passed her house again. When he got
home the president was on TV describing offensive nuclear missiles on the *imprisoned island* of Cuba. Paulie's little brother Angie
imitated Kennedy's voice until his mother told him to hush. The
handsome man's face was haggard, the eyelids swollen, lizard-like.
These missiles would make it possible for the Soviets to vaporize
major U.S. cities in minutes. The president's pompadour wagged
up and down as he spoke. He said that our armed forces were prepared for *any eventuality,* and that a missile fired from Cuba would
result in a *full retaliatory nuclear strike on the Soviet Union.*

Oh, my God in heaven, Paulie's mother said.

The missile crisis lasted six days, and each day a larger crowd
gathered before the appliance store in Berkeley, college students

THE ÏSLANDS OF DIVINE MUSIC

and working people on break among the neighborhood winos. Mrs. Rinaldi's face was pale, her eyes swollen in class. She told him to stay after, placed her hand on his arm, and asked if he knew where she lived.

The Cadillac was gone. Paulie's heart bounced against his sternum as he walked to her door. She had changed to a blouse and culottes, which Paulie took for a very short skirt until she turned and led him through the house.

Stern faces of dead relatives scowled from the mantel. A marlin encased in laminate stared as he followed her out the back to a small iron door leaning at forty-five degrees into a hump of earth behind the house. Mrs. Rinaldi lifted the latch and swung the door open. He followed her down a ladder into a concrete chamber buried under the dandelions.

She had him carry five-gallon drums filled with drinking water, boxes filled with canned food, blankets and pillows, candles and Sterno. After several trips they sat together on a canvas cot wiping their brows and breathing the dank air. Do you have one of these?

Paulie said they didn't. Mrs. Rinaldi sat beside him in the semi-darkness and said she hadn't been this frightened since the Nazi bombs, the many nights of her childhood spent in terror waiting for death to drop from the sky. Paulie only vaguely understood what she referred to. Black-and-white newsreels of buildings reduced to rubble, bomber pilots holding their thumbs up. This is really so much worse, she said, because if neither side backs down . . . Her voice trailed off.

Paulie sat a moment wishing the sirens would sound. He remembered all the drills in elementary school, his head resting on his knees, the children under desks with eyes closed, waiting. A rocket with an atomic bomb on its way to San Francisco, the blast so bright even from across the bay he would see through his eyelids, he would see the bones in his legs. He wished for the screaming civil defense sirens and maybe just one bomb hitting New York, so that he and Mrs. Rinaldi would have to wait it out together. His family would drive to the shelter under the library, and if San Francisco did get hit the fallout would blow south to Los Angeles. Pete, drunk on some park bench in the city, would be vaporized.

Their elbows and knees touched. He listened to her breathe. They would share the water and canned soup, listen to his little radio for war updates. To conserve power they'd lie together in the dark, on this little cot.

Did you hear that, what is that? She climbed the ladder, and Paulie stood beneath her, weak with lust. A droning engine noise grew louder and louder. Mrs. Rinaldi reached into the sunlight, her arms flailing, and pulled the door closed.

He had never been in such total darkness. Her voice trembled in the space above him. He could feel the heat of her legs in front of his face. Help me down, please, help me. It sounded like she was crying.

His hands touched her buttocks by mistake and swiftly slid up to her waist. She stepped down, slowly, into his arms. She trembled, and he felt moisture where her face pressed against his shoulder. What was it?

A huge plane, a military plane. She sobbed. Pardon me, I'm a mess.

Probably from Travis AFB.

I must find the light switch. Oh, dear. He felt her body pivot from his embrace without entirely disengaging. Travis what did you say?

An American military base. The light came on, a single glaring bulb hung from the ceiling. Her face was pale and blotched, her cheeks shining with tears. Mrs. Rinaldi, if the Russians drop a bomb, it won't be by plane.

Oh, of course not. She sat on the cot. Oh, I'm silly, aren't I? Oh, Christ.

In the movies of that time, a man would give a hysterical woman a glass of liquor to settle her nerves. Paulie searched the plywood shelf filled with colorful labels, tomato-vegetable soup, Spam, flashlight batteries, until he spotted a brandy bottle. The shelter was so snug he was able to reach it without moving from the cot. Would you like some of this?

She laughed. No, thank you. I think we were saving that for . . . well, for some comfort.

I love you.

She stared at him. He thought he had only said this to himself, the way he would chant prayers and encouragements during games when his family was around, but the words had slipped out. Oh, my, she said. You mustn't.

I mustn't.

She climbed the ladder. He sat on the cot and listened to her grunt softly. He was an idiot, a child. He heard her gasp. Paul, you try this. She came down, and he got up slowly, then climbed to where she'd been. It was over. Push, Paul. The door wouldn't open. He shoved and shook it. Is there some kind of handle? he asked.

She climbed up beside him. He was pressed against her backside. Push, Paul, hard as you can. They pushed together.

I think it's latched on the outside, he said. It must have fallen in place when you closed it.

Oh, my God! Oh, goddamn my idiot husband! This is the most ridiculous door! She bounced up and down against him, pushing, and her hair brushed his face, and he wanted to stay right where he was for hours and inhale the smoke and perfume in her hair, even though he mustn't. He figured Pete would open the door eventually because they'd left such an obvious trail: the open back door, the missing supplies from the back porch. Oh, this is ingenious! You survive the blast only to starve to death in a crypt!

They lay together under the wool blankets. She wanted to be held, and after they kissed once she said, Please, just hold me, and he did. Hours passed. He inserted the nipple into her ear when she asked, pressing it carefully into the delicate shell of her flesh, and she lay breathless beside him, taking in a conveyance new to her, though she was seventeen years his senior. He could feel the difference in her breathing when she took it in, as she listened to the talk of missiles lying atop ships, swaying over the black ocean.

She fell asleep, and he turned off the light. Russian merchant vessels approached the American battleships surrounding Cuba. His life as a schoolboy was over. He knew that if one should pierce that

circle and reach the island a terrible new life would begin. Cities il-
luminated by white flames, families incinerated while he and this
woman remained safe underground, waiting to emerge into their
new lives. He knew that if the crisis passed he should join the service, that he should take what grace he'd had on the field and make
a life of protecting loved ones from communists and Nazis. He held
her and thought of the end of this life and the start of another and
fell into a dream of chasing a ball across the outfield of Seals Stadium. He was dressed in baggy pinstripes which flapped like pajamas as he ran, and his glove was fat and barely larger than his hand.
The grandstands were filled with his classmates and family, even
those who had passed away, and they wore black suits and round
hats like immigrants gathered on a ship. He was reaching for the
ball, struggling to lift his legs in the heavy garment, when he woke
in the dark, and they were moving against each other, sliding out of
their clothes. He felt her hand on his back, and they moved with
each other and into each other until she cried out and the brilliant
light of day exploded above them.

THE CITY OF ROCKS AT THE END OF THE WORLD

Penelope

O f his youth she knew only sketchy details. Penelope learned from the old woman, Rosanidia, that Jesús and his teenaged mother had left the city to pick artichokes near Salinas after old Giuseppe, Penny's grandfather, had died. She heard rumors about Maria and the evil men from her past, drug pushers and criminals, men who had stalked her like wolves until Giuseppe had taken her in. Her mother and aunts defended Maria against all allegations, agreeing with Rosanidia, who called her *pobrecita*, or a poor little thing. Her father and Uncle Ludovico shook their heads or smirked, and sometimes used the word *tramp* instead of *thing*.

In the years that followed Jesús and Maria's flight from San Francisco, Rosanidia received cards from places with quaint names: Hood River, Vale, Nampa, Rupert, and she showed them to Penny and her Aunt Francesca. The old ladies touched each other's arms and waved their hands as they shaped the words in Spanish, Italian, and English. Penny puzzled through the language and gestures of the women as they described the travels of the mother and child.

Her catechism teacher said that they'd probably *joined the migrant stream,* and in Penny's imagination they were carried away by a wide brown river through the valleys of California, floating to faraway fields where the earth provided sustenance and the Romans and Pharisees from her Sunday missal couldn't persecute them. At night, before drifting to sleep, she'd picture herself joining them, floating in the soft water and the sweet winds of summer to some fragrant field where they would embrace and eat their fill of strawberries, where she would hold the toddler on her hip in a field of wildflowers and laugh.

She remembered how men's heads turned like owls' when Maria walked down a street, and how women's faces opened up when they saw the child. Their beauty was palpable; it changed the temperature of a room when they walked in. It started a quivering in the air the way a sudden rhythm-and-blues beat could make her dance before she realized what she was doing.

Two years after their flight Rosanidia gave Francesca a post-office-box number in a place called Jerome. Penny wrote Maria a letter in what she thought was simple enough English for Maria to read. She dotted her "i"s with circles and ended each sentence with an exclamation point. She asked about the orchards and fields, the mountains and valleys. She asked if the baby was in kindergarten or first grade. She described her cantankerous math teacher and sent one of her wallet-sized school portraits.

Maria and Jesús were living in a former internment camp used to contain Japanese Americans during World War II. Mexican families crowded together in old barracks without hot water, usually six people to a ten-by-twenty-foot room. The camp was circled by barbed-wire fencing, and the nearest store was several miles away, across an expanse of desert sagebrush. An enormous potato-processing plant filled the air with a perpetual stink. Few of the children made it to school.

Of his youth Penny could only imagine something sweet and bucolic, a life spent running in fields and swimming in rivers, days spent eating the fruit just picked from the tree. She imagined their poverty as something simple, a one-room cabin in an orchard, a canvas tent in fragrant fields. When her mother told her they might be living in squalor and that her father should send them money, she pictured squatters living in happy squalor, claiming a piece of God's earth by the simple act of bending their knees in a clearing near a river. The word *squalor* suggested to her a free and sloppy life, like her bedroom before her mother made her pick it up, a way of living outside society's rules. In poverty people lived by God's blessing, she thought, and in squalor most anything out of the ordinary could happen.

In Maria and Jesús's squalid quarters the crucifix above the sheet-metal stove was plastic, and the savior's feet were accordingly disfigured by years of fire. Little Jesús knelt before its warmth and ate the animal cookies from the box. He could see the first sunlight touch the blond-and-silver foothills of the Sawtooth Range through a window cracked and mended by masking tape. He was awaiting his first day of school, during which he would sit with two other Mexican children, lost in a dust devil of unintelligible English.

Maria was sick of the camp and the potato and beet fields, the bitter cold and isolation, the stinking wind which tore their clothes from the line. There were lines penciled in Japanese on bed slats, words written from a grief of twenty years before; there were cracks in the walls that let the cold in, and rats that bred under the floorboards. While Jesús would spend his first day lost in a classroom she would find a niche in a motel on the highway, and soon they would live in a room with plumbing, two beds, a hot plate, and a TV. Maria would earn rent on her back and by cleaning rooms, and Jesús would watch Roy Rogers while she sold herself in a vacant room to drunk campesinos and cowboys as well as the Mormon businessmen who ran the city council and school board. Maria would drink the sugary wine that Arturo, the motel manager and pimp, provided her, and in a year she'd gain thirty pounds, yammering at the TV about God's plan to end the world while Jesús, sitting beside her on the bed, tried to decipher the jokes on the sitcoms.

His schoolmates called him Chuy and sometimes Indio because he was dark and looked more Indian than the others. He was swift-footed and clever, a rascal with a big laugh whom older boys chased but couldn't catch on the playground. He was often in trouble for drawing instead of adding, speaking Spanish where it wasn't allowed, and climbing all over the classroom as if it were a jungle gym. He loved the classroom and the kids and the teacher, even when he was in trouble. Miss Rawlings was a young woman fresh out of the normal school in Albion, and Jesús was her first challenge, a monolingual urchin who wouldn't sit still, a boy with a huge smile and beautiful hair. She drove to the motel room to discuss Jesús's behavior on a bitter January evening, and it was all she could do to restrain herself from scooping him off the bed, where he sat eating potato chips and watching *The Honeymooners,* and taking him home. Miss Rawlings sat beside him for twenty minutes among the empty wine bottles and butt-filled ashtrays, watching Ralph Cramden threaten to punch his wife and send her to the moon, until Maria appeared. She had just finished servicing a client, and her hair was wild, and she smelled of wine and a man's sweat and semen.

Mrs. Verbicaro? The young woman stood to shake hands.

Very little was communicated between the two women, mostly because Maria was nearly dumbstruck. To think that a handsome woman of Miss Rawlings's age could be childless and a teacher! She kept stealing glances at the nice clothing and pert hairdo of the young woman as she made an effort to tidy the room. Taped to a mirror beside the TV was Penny's picture, a grinning fourteen-year-old with bangs and a pimple on her nose, a mouth whose adult incisors were too big to keep inside, whose joy was too big to contain. It would remain there the few years that Jesús and Maria would spend at the Top Hat Motel while Penny grew into her adult figure and Miss Rawlings became familiar enough with her fiancé's lust to realize what that smell had been when Jesús's mother had walked into the room.

or Penny the idea of Jesús and Maria became fainter and, at the same time, more idealized. She would sit in class staring out the window at distant oaks and picture the mother in robes and a head scarf carrying the swaddled infant beneath the trees. She couldn't remember what they looked like anymore, and so they became dark and beautiful shapes moving among the trees, kneeling at distant creeks like deer, rustling with the leaves outside her window at night. About once a year she would write a letter to them, wondering if they ever received her words since she'd never gotten a response. When she thought of Idaho she pictured deep evergreen forests, not the beige-colored high desert where the mother and child lived.

Jesús would find himself cornered by Mormons in the grammar school, cheerful young men with crew cuts and skinny neckties who'd invite him to play checkers and basketball at their church. These men would invariably ask him about his home life and whether or not he was part of an Indian tribe. By his third year in school he understood almost everything the Mormons said to him, except for a reference to a tribe of Laminites, which sounded like something the librarian liked to do. One of the men even said that he, Jesús, was a Laminite, which made him a cut above a Mexican, in terms of redemption.

What if my dad was Italian, hey?

Not good, the young man said. You need to be Indian.

One night Jesús and Maria sat before the set until Arturo

knocked. Beyond the old man's shoulder were the distant sounds of hooting and a kind of growling laughter, like the noises some hybrid of man and dog might make. Maria told Jesús to wait, and he sat through two shows before he got anxious. He stuck his head out the door, into the frigid night air. Something was next to the snow-covered, stunted hedge, some bundle of clothes which, after Jesús's eyes got accustomed to the dark, seemed to have a head attached to it. Jesús called out, then made his way across the snow to Arturo, who had a black skein of blood on his face. The child yelled for his mother and ran from door to door, finding one of them ajar. Maria was in that room, lying on her stomach aslant a bed. Her dress was torn up to her neck, and there was blood on her legs and buttocks.

His howling brought Yvonne, the bovine redhead who, until that evening, had never spoken a word to Maria or Jesús. Yvonne had three grown boys who spent much of their time in various correctional institutions or on the rodeo circuit, and she had recently moved to the Top Hat from a trailer behind a Truax truck stop, where she'd waited tables and performed fellatio on truckers. She'd seen the three cowboys earlier that evening and told Arturo no dice because Yvonne could spot mean little shitkickers a mile off. Holy fucking mother of God, she said when she rushed into the room.

Yvonne had just drawn only one eyebrow onto her shaved forehead, and her bathrobe was unfastened. She lifted Jesús onto her hip, and tears gushed out of her eyes and smeared her makeup as she blabbered about what she should do, casting her thoughts aloud above the sound of the child's weeping. She set the boy down, and the two of them turned Maria onto her back and shook her back to consciousness. Moaning softly, Maria opened her eyes and hugged her child. Yvonne stomped out into the snow and dragged Arturo into the room, blubbering and talking to herself the entire time. She placed a motel towel on the gash in his head, and Arturo came around and started cursing in Spanish.

Maria had a mild concussion as well as a lesion in her colon where the cowboys had shoved a broom handle. Despite the rambling explanations Yvonne offered, this cruelty was a bitter mystery to Jesús. Moreover, the subject was off-limits after that evening. Maria and Arturo each spent a week in bed attended by Arturo's cousin Esperanza. Yvonne moved back to the trailer behind the truck stop and never spoke to them again. Neither the police nor medical authorities were called; the assailants were sons of old families in the valley. Whenever Jesús brought it up, he was silenced.

Of course Penny had no sense of the life the child and his mother lived, though her thoughts returned to them every so often, especially during Sunday mass. The old story of the migrant stream, of a life following the crops of the American breadbasket, became more somber after she'd read Steinbeck. She wondered if Maria's beautiful shoulders were now disfigured by years of stoop labor, or if the boy had become bitter with poverty.

Mormon missionaries on the playground, Catholic sisters from the church where the Mexican people went, and a couple of teachers knew that things weren't right at home for Jesús. They prayed for him. They gossiped about the mother. He learned to avoid answering their questions directly and to respond tersely, or sometimes with aphorisms he'd piece together, using a bit of each idiom from home and school. Well, that's how the tree falls, *no?* From such sticks you get such splinters, *que no?* When it rains, you get wet, *y que?*

He learned to read English, mostly by poring over Arturo's old *National Enquirer*s, and years later he found Penny's letters, which Maria had never been able to read. The latest one, written nearly two years before Jesús read it, described Penny's first days of a high school year. Jesús read it several times, enjoying the long sentences which cataloged the many events in the girl's big-city school, the rallies and football games, the dances with local rock-and-roll musicians, an assembly featuring some hootenanny singers. He enjoyed her descriptions of the disaster drills, how the girls in their long, tight dresses had to bend their knees enough to fit under their desks, how the Russians were building so many atom bombs that Penny's dad was considering digging a bomb shelter in the backyard. He decided to write back, and one of the young missionaries helped him address the letter. All he could think of to say was a thank-you, along with a brief response to her thoughts about the atom bomb. His mother had always spoken of mass destruction, of God's plan to end the world, and Jesús had often imagined the various ways the world might end in flames and floods and explosions. He wrote to Penny: *Thank You! With atom bombs I think only God drops the Big One, and that's the way the ball jumps, no?*

Penny was in her room listening to Dion and the Belmonts and graphing some coordinate geometry when her brother Angelo barged in and threw the letter at her. Angelo was always first at the mailbox those days because he awaited some quasi-pornographic novelty his parents didn't know about, and he enjoyed barging in on his siblings and startling them with some weird noise or impression he'd create. This time he imitated President Kennedy: Um, Miss Verbicaro? You seem to have received a message from Cubar or Chinar.

There was no return address, and Penny's name was scrawled in pencil. She had no idea who it was from, or why some kid would write to her about the bomb. Maybe some weird elementary school project? She returned to her math while Angelo hung over her shoulder. Is it from the communists, Miss Verbicaro? It looks like a communist stamp, Miss Verbicaro. I think it's Cubar.

Mr. President, get lost. She looked at the stamp and the postmark, which had *Ida* on it, then she shoved it aside.

Maria took a job waiting tables at a cowboy bar called the Five-Ten Club, where she got decent tips only when she wore a low-cut blouse and let men place their hands on her. Arturo rarely asked her to service clients at the Top Hat after the assault, so she cleaned a few rooms for rent and occasionally crawled into his bed while Jesús was at school. He would twist open a bottle of Ripple wine to share, and they would watch a quiz show while she placed her hands on his lap and lectured him about the end of the world, which was imminent.

A storm hit the Western states that fall, knocking down redwoods and Douglas fir, snapping power lines, and leaving Jesús and Maria in the dark for two days. It brought a torrent of rain to Northern California and stopped the World Series in San Francisco. Penny thought of writing to Maria about it, describing the flooded neighborhoods along the bay front and the day she and her father had to cross San Pablo Avenue with the water up to the car doors. Then she picked up the child's letter and realized from whom it had come.

She began a letter in response to Jesús's words, thinking that he must be an odd little boy to write the things he had written. She asked about his mother and sent a news clipping about the flooding in the Bay Area. She described crossing San Pablo Avenue in the high water.

Jesús read the letter by candle because the power was down again. He was thinking of writing a response one day when Arturo stumbled into their room stinking drunk and shouting about the Russians and the end of the world. According to the old man, the country was about to go to war and, with the help of the Russians, blow up the world. Maria started packing.

It was October 23, 1962. Arturo drove them through town with the car radio squawking war from the metal dash, and he and Jesús tried to translate for Maria. Before the appliance store on Main there was a traffic jam of pickup trucks and old sedans, and people were standing beside their vehicles or on the sidewalk watching the TV in the window. Jesús saw the president's handsome face in the window for a second before Arturo maneuvered the car to an Esso station. There they waited, among a cluster of fuel hoarders, to fill the tank.

The old man wiped tears with his sleeve and guided the car drunkenly across the desert, aided now and then by Maria's hand on the wheel when he drifted across the line. From the faint radio waves traveling hundreds of miles from Salt Lake or Boise to the old

Ford, Jesús heard that the Russians were getting closer and closer to Cuba just as the jalopy bounced farther and farther across the sage desert and onto a narrow gravel road. Huge, pale-faced men in fur hats guided dark warships from their frozen shores, sliced across the ocean toward an island where Latinos like them were brainwashed slaves who denounced God. The dark ships were weighted down with missiles nearly as large as the vessels themselves, and the communists wanted to set these death rockets in Cuba, where they'd be close enough to hit America easily and start a war to end the world.

They drove on washboard gravel until a rock formation came into view, a granite batholith rising out of the desert like an island in the sea. In a circle of boulders and broken beer bottles they parked under the bullet-pocked sign: *City of Rocks.*

They used the decrepit outhouses and slung their things over their shoulders. Not five minutes up the trail Arturo fell to his knees, in a clamor of bottles and Spam tins, and wept. He asked forgiveness from God and his mother for all the awful things he'd done. Abandoning his wife and children in Mexico and promoting prostitution were among the many sins he wanted to get off his chest before the end of the world. He told the others to go on without him, that he would return to the car to wait it out because he was too old and sick and rotten with sin. Maria made the sign of the cross and told him to go with God. She and Jesús climbed into the massive rock formation while Arturo went with God back to the brown '52 Ford, opened another bottle of Ripple, and passed out in the backseat. The sun set.

Under a cliff, in a cleft of rock which was not exactly the cave

Maria had envisioned, mother and child huddled in their motel blankets. Jesús had never seen rock like this, smooth but jagged at the crags, polished granite with veins of quartz. He looked at the stars of light in the rock, and later he looked at the stars themselves, the black sky thick with them, cloudy with them, alive with them. A shooting star crossed the sky, and they gasped and clung to each other. Then Maria pointed out a faint orange glow above a rim of distant mountains. Though it probably indicated the city lights of Pocatello, she said that this was a burning city struck by a bomb, hundreds of kilometers away, and that they should cover their mouths and noses with the blankets so as not to breathe the poison.

The next morning Maria heated beans over a can of Sterno. Jesús unfolded a piece of paper and began his letter to Penny. He used a flat boulder as a table and gazed into the pinnacles of rock as he thought about what to say.

Ten days later Penny received a letter written in a bumpy scrawl. *We are in the city of rocks at the end of the world,* it began. *if the world is all* destruido *you probable can't get this letter. Mama says the peoples in santo francisco will probable boil like chickens in a pot so the meat comes off the bone. I am sorry for you with much heart. We see the city burn far over the mountains and cry for the peoples. well. Arturo stay behind in the ford and might cook like meat in a can or maybe not. You live all sins and you die like spam in a* lata que no?

Once again, Jesús's words left Penny dumbfounded. Was he just a weird little boy? Was he precocious or mentally unstable? The letter continued in smoother printing, apparently written some days later and on a better surface:

Well we are home we walk all day for that arturo leave and mama is much in anger. The world is not over and I am happy you are fine and me tambien, well it's the way the wiener wobbles. Mama says we will soon leave this place for good. With much love I hope you are happy. Even in the city of rocks many brite flowers find a place to grow.

On a cool November evening seven years later Penny stood before a Mexican bakery in San Francisco. A group of sugar skulls peeked from the windows of a hacienda made of dough or gingerbread. She knew enough Spanish to translate the icing on the building: *Dia de los Muertos,* Day of the Dead. It made her think of the six days when death had hung so close to them all, her mother sitting before the TV, her brother in some silent world of his own, her father when Paulie had joined the marines, and how unreal that time seemed now, after its passage, compared with the very real and daily reports of death from Vietnam, with the real problems in their lives. As she stood before the plate glass she imagined the baby and his mother peering from a window in a city made of stone, an ancient city carved into a cliff, leaning at the end of the world.

Penny had only heard from Jesús twice in those last seven years, and the last letters she'd sent had come back unopened. Mother and child had been on the move, mostly in the Rocky Mountain states and the Great Basin, in desolate towns full of work crews, oil fields, mining operations, dam construction. Penny didn't know Jesús had taken up his drunk mother's burden and, at the age of twelve, sneaked into taverns with her, dressed in her clothes, in order to take men's money. He was a convincing trans-

vestite, a slim-hipped Latin beauty with scarlet lipstick and tur-
quoise eyeliner, and it amazed him how easily these men, who spent
months in danger and drudgery in order to mail money home to
their wives, who spent all day sweating and moving machines with
their callused hands, could be fooled into stuffing ten-dollar bills
into his. And then there were the men who saw through the cos-
tume and called him a queer and paid to enter him from behind. For
Jesús there was that sudden frightening violation with its attendant
thrill of pain and its disgusting pleasure mixed with the pain. There
was a debasement and acceptance of what is most dirty and wrong
and deeply pleasurable about being a human being, that most basic
giving over of himself to another. He was a queer. He was something men fucked and told jokes about and talked about lining up
against a wall and shooting, ridding the world of them. One evening
their cruelty nearly killed him, much in the way it had nearly killed
his mother: he was stripped and sexually assaulted, then beaten and
left for dead in a parking lot.

Penny waited for the electric Muni to take her to San Francisco
State College, where she taught composition writing as a gradu-
ate student. She had combed her long, wavy hair onto the kitchen
counter of her flat in Noe Valley and ironed it straight. She had
drunk two cups of coffee and shared two joints of marijuana with
her boyfriend, Charles, who said that the straightening accentuated
Penny's vulnerable angularity and made her look like a ghost with
sunken eyes and a Roman nose. Charles was a self-professed Yippie

and revolutionary trying to find the right organization to identify with, and he'd spent time in meetings with the SDS, Peace and Freedom Party, SLA, Weather Underground, Patriot Party, Diggers, and recently a Black Panther support group called the Motherfuckers, but he still hadn't found the right fit. Penny didn't tell Charles her class didn't meet that evening, that she was going instead to a *conscious breathing* class taught by one of her ex-lovers, a past-life-regression therapist and parking-lot attendant named Frank.

Charles had a low opinion of most of the classes offered at San Francisco State through the Experimental College unless they had to do with revolution, and his impression of Frank and consciousness-raising in general was lower still. Penny didn't vocally disagree with Charles, but a lot of reading and talk about the boundaries of consciousness, as well as recent experiences with marijuana and LSD, had made her feel receptive to an intuitive journey which seemed accessible through the simple act of breathing, and the course, after two meetings, was going well. Also, Frank was cute, and things just presented themselves to her lately when she practiced his breathing technique, the coincidence of a word repeated, a snippet from some song with special significance. The Mexican bakery display seemed a portent, a little message from God, reinforced by the synchronous appearance of the word *Idaho* floating past her feet on the side of a windblown french fries sack. Penny boarded the Muni and closed her eyes to concentrate on her breathing. She saw faces: her grandfather's on the day he died, her mother's the day of her parents' divorce, her brother Paulie's in the U.S. Marine Corps portrait on the mantel.

Death had passed over Paulie, but not without leaving its mark: he'd returned home that year dishonorably discharged and addicted to heroin. He was now living in a wino hotel south of Market, wandering to and from his methadone treatments at the mission and drinking quart bottles of ale with a couple of other vets on a park bench. His hair had grown out, and he was always dressed in an old military coat which reeked of booze and smoke and sweat. With his bushy beard and wild eyes he scared Penny and gave her the impression of Rasputin or Charles Manson in a Giants baseball cap and glasses. Whenever she saw him she wanted to flee his presence, to make sure he didn't know where she lived, which was less than two miles from his hotel.

Jesús was less than a mile from her at that moment. He had run away and come to San Francisco, as had thousands of teenagers that year. One night he'd watched his mother stagger around the room in a red negligee stained orange at the armpits and then looked at himself in the mirror, his long black hair and feminine affect so much like hers, and the next morning he'd said his farewell and stood on the highway with his thumb out. He found his way to the city and ingested hallucinogens and made money for a month panhandling and turning sexual favors on the streets where his mother had done the same many years before, until one evening, when he stood on the bridge staring east toward the lighthouse on Alcatraz, he juggled the idea of jumping. There was a way to end suffering, and it really took no effort to achieve this, just a simple act of letting go, and there was something tremendously seductive in the music of that gesture of stepping onto the rail and dropping toward

the little island and the black water, something comforting in knowing that this was available to him, this means of breaking the circle
of pain. And the pain was his beautiful mother dying slowly from
booze and despair, her swollen face the day he'd left, and the pain
was a man pressing too deep inside him, and the pain was the endless fields stripped bare and lifeless under the machinery of stupe-
fied work crews, and the pain was the desperate children like him
come to escape their lives in the city of love. The choice to live
came down to a coin toss, a chance sign, a gull drifting above him
among the bridge wires. If the bird flies to the right, I jump, he said
to himself. To the left, I walk back.

Penny breathed deeply into her thoughts. She had the sensation
of taking breath into the hidden places of her being, as if there were
pulmonary recesses which housed memory, a grandfather falling
dead, a beautiful child running on the beach, a brother whose mind
was wounded by war, a darkly handsome father who'd left her
mother for a woman near her own age. As she worked to let her
body relax on the nearly empty vessel, staying aware of the spinning
wheels on the rails and the whistling brakes, she saw, among the images of memory, a garish image of Jesus Christ from her aunt's cal-
endar. This Jesus had a wrestler's muscular neck and a halo floating
above his orange-brown hair at a slight angle, like a glowing UFO
banking for a turn. A confectionary neon heart shone like a wild-
cherry cough drop through his breast. Penny laughed and opened
her eyes just as the streetcar stopped.

A young person with a dark face, with prominent cheeks and
lustrous black hair falling across them in a feminine way, leaned

against a lamppost just beyond her window. Male or female in the loose blouse and harem pants, she couldn't tell, but there was something beautiful and familiar in this person's face. Through the glass their eyes met, and Penny's heart jumped, and as the pneumatic door snapped shut and the car lurched forward she mouthed his name, and he nodded. Both of them opened their mouths and pointed as the train swiftly drew them apart, the one who had stood on the Golden Gate Bridge an hour earlier and decided against death by the direction of a bird's flight and the other who'd returned in thought to that hidden mesa at the end of the world where a mother and child huddled under a blue poncho and waited for the shadow of death to pass over.

MISTER SANTA CLAUS

Mickey

Michelle Verbicaro, always called Mickey by everybody all her life, had an extra chromosome and a puppy with the same name as the president's wife. She had a sister in college, a brother in the marines, and a funny older brother and baby sister who still lived at home. Mickey had the slightly Asiatic eyes, round face, and slumped shoulders of most people with Down syndrome, and she had thick, lustrous black hair which her mother kept trimmed in a bowl cut, and a laugh which was so contagious that an usher at the Oaks Theater in Berkeley often warned the projectionist to adjust the volume whenever Mickey arrived for a matinee.

One Saturday in the last month of the year, between the two turkey dinners, Mickey and Lady-Bird sneaked out for a walk while her mother was at the Lucky Store, and they talked the entire way about Mr. Santa Claus, who would be holding children on his lap at Hink's and listening to them speak of whatever their hearts desired. Mickey's heart had a big list, and this would be a special Christmas with the whole family there, and she had photographs of herself over the years sitting on Santa's lap, but none since she'd reached age fourteen because of a rule her mother had told her about, which she considered a dopy rule. She walked through her neighborhood of stucco houses in El Cerrito, past her Aunt Francesca's and Nona Rosari's and the homes of about seven other aunts and cousins, to the north edge of Berkeley.

It was a gray day with occasional showers, just Mickey and Lady-Bird's favorite walking weather because nothing felt better when you were trudging along than a cold rain on your face. They made it to the top of Solano Avenue, where the theater was, and continued the only way Mickey knew to go, which was through the streetcar tunnel. This scared Lady-Bird so much that Mickey had to carry her. By the time they made it to the downtown Mickey's feet were sore, so she took off her shoes and soaked her feet in a gutter which flowed with rainwater and hot-dog wrappers.

Mr. Santa Claus looked regal and thrilling at the end of the line of kids and parents in the opulent department store, but when she got closer she thought he'd lost weight and a certain spunk over the years. His eyes darted back and forth as her turn approached. He laughed without the big, throaty ho-ho-ho. When her turn came he put his hands up the way you let a dog know you won't bite them if they won't bite you, and his voice sounded like one of her dad's friends' at the card table late at night, kind of mean and impatient. No way, he said. You are too big and too . . . huge, in fact. This is for the little guys. You wanna break my kneecaps, Cookie? So solly. No can do. Please make room for the next customer.

Lady-Bird was licking her own pee-hole when Mickey came

out to the sidewalk, bawling, wishing she were as small as Lady-Bird herself. The two of them started for home and got a ride from her cousin Susan, who, among three other relatives, had been driving around for hours looking for her. Holy smoke, what happened, Mickey-Wicky? You're soaked to the skin!

Mickey told her about Santa Claus, and Susan called Santa something which she'd never heard from a girl cousin, and she drove fast to Mickey's house. Mickey's mother's eyes were like a raccoon's when she ran up to hug her, and her mom and cousin were both crying with her and now and then saying mad things about Santa when her father, Joe, came home and said, Let me take care of this.

Joe had just left Spenger's Fish Grotto, where he and the secretary from a local hardware store, Julie, had spent an hour with her hand on his leg talking about business. It felt good to have a legitimate reason to leave the house before his wife could ask him why he avoided her eyes and smelled of booze and scampi, and he drove to Hink's and spoke with the manager, who called Santa from his chair to an office upstairs. Yeah? Santa said.

Bernie, the manager said, I'm sorry. Listen, Bernie, I thought you should talk with this gentleman.

Joe apologized before he told Santa that he'd apparently made his daughter, who was mentally a little slow, cry. Maybe it was the way he'd spoken to her?

Santa didn't seem to know what he was talking about at first, but then he sort of remembered this huge retarded girl, all right.

Joe could smell the sour beer and mustard on the guy's breath. I'm supposed to hold giant retards on my lap? Santa asked the manager.

Calm down, Bernie. The manager wiped his brow with a handkerchief.

Joe sized Santa up. Even through the cotton beard and padded velvet suit he could see that the guy was about ten years his junior, but Joe figured he could cut the suds-guzzling smart aleck in half with a couple of punches. I'm not your employer, he said, but if I was I'd kick your ass with your last paycheck right now.

Santa told him to perform an impossible sex act upon himself, and his black gloves at the ends of the furry white cuffs made fists. The manager, a nervous, balding man, stepped between them. Joe smiled and very slowly took off his sport coat and rolled his sleeves to the elbow. He held his chin up and smiled, and while his feet slid into the stance he'd boxed from years ago, his hands remained open, beckoning. Come on, he thought, give me your best shot, Fat Man. The manager convinced Santa that it was time for him to get back to work, but not before the man in the stuffed red suit had compared Joe to a part of the human anatomy used in excretion.

That guy is an embarrassment to Christmas. Joe put his coat back on.

He's a nephew to one of the owners, the manager said.

Ah. Joe thought of his brothers, Narciso and Ludovico, one thick as a fence post, the other about as calm as a bantam rooster. I'm sorry. He's going to get a candy cane up his ass if he's not careful.

The manager laughed and mopped his brow.

The world was spinning off-kilter for Joe of late, and it wasn't just the gin and tonics from the fish grotto or the fact that he'd been an inch from getting into a fight with Kris Kringle. Sometimes he would cruise along the freeway and imagine how simple it would be to let the wheel drift a little and plow into a concrete wall. Sometimes the only thing in the world which made him happy was the only thing which made him want to drive his car through concrete at sixty miles an hour, and that was his attraction to Julie, a woman barely older than his daughter Penny.

A decade earlier he had counted himself among the luckiest of men, but something about the mid-'60s gave him a feeling of disgust and exhilaration at the same time. He tried to figure this out as he crept through the downtown traffic, and he took a long detour in order to figure some more. Hell, he wasn't hungry, anyway, and sometimes sitting at the dinner table made him nauseated. Mickey had an excuse for eating like a slob, but Angelo, who was now in high school, was the worst, especially when they ate at Joe's mother's with the whole clan. Maybe it was that his first two, his beautiful oldest girl and his quiet, athletic son, were both gone from the house. More than that, one was now an angry college student who hung out with long-haired beatniks while her brother, Joe's pride and joy, had lost the light of happiness in his face.

That was it, he thought: they were a couple of sobersides, and the few times he'd seen them in the past three years neither one of them had been able to laugh. Of course they were sitting on opposite sides of the fence, and if you believed the papers they had a lot of company on each side of that fence, but one thing Joe had realized about living, and this was something which Julie had helped him realize, was that if you can't get a kick out of it now and then you may as well give it up. A lifetime of being the serious one in a family of loud laughers and wine drinkers, of being the guy who worried about every yard of material and every margin of profit for an extended family which reaped the benefits of his fretting, had brought him to this point at midlife where he felt obliged to live it up now and then. Get out and dance at one of those damned go-go places Julie liked. Take a weekend at South Tahoe with the brothers and slip away to meet Julie for lunch.

Okay, the lying was a big piece of his feeling off-kilter. His pop had chased women and ended up living with a little Mexican whore his last couple of years, and Joe always used the old man as the yardstick of negative integers in the measure of a man, but here he was spending time with a girl who didn't know who Douglas MacArthur or Benny Goodman were. Although it was still just friendship, it confused the hell out of him. That love was a messy thing, that it didn't always play by the rules, was common coinage of the times, particularly this era of bushy sideburns and short skirts, but it didn't take the sting away from Joe's duplicity, and it didn't help him understand his love for his oldest children, which had nothing messy about it now but felt frozen and out of grasp.

The house resonated with Burl Ives singing about a little drummer boy, and even this popular carol seemed off-track to Joe. Mary nodded, barrumpapumpum, the ox's ass kept time, barrumpapumpum? He wouldn't say that, would he? There seemed to be a new liberality in common language which struck Joe between the eyes now and then. People said things on TV you would have heard only in a locker room a few years earlier. Billboards looked pornographic. As Joe stepped inside he heard a high-pitched, whining cry weave itself into the music, and as he entered the living room a soldier stood up from the couch and extended his hand. It was his son.

Hey! Joe reached to give him a hug. He felt stiff, all sinew and bone, and his face looked gaunt and bruised around the eyes.

Dad.

How's it going, Tiger?

All right.

How much time off did Uncle give you?

A month.

That's great!

I'm only here a couple of days, though. What's eating Mickey?

For a moment Joe was at a loss for words. His wife, Mary Louise, stepped into the room and told the Santa Claus story, including the part about Joe's going downtown to talk with the manager. Mickey's whining underscored the nasal voice on the phonograph record.

Joe started to tell them both how close he had been to fistfighting with Kris Kringle, but his son's last words kept interfering with his thoughts. A couple of days out of a month? A horn sounded in their driveway, and Paulie stepped briskly to the door. These were some buddies who wanted him to show them around Frisco, he told his parents.

You're not going to eat at your grandmother's?

Probably not, Mom. I told these guys I'd show them Frisco, and they're going to show me Dago and Ensenada.

Paulie, what the hell do you mean, Dago?

Dad, that's San Diego. I'll be back tonight.

Burl Ives kept crooning about that goddamned drummer boy playing his nuts off for Jesus as Joe watched his son climb into a green car filled with boys in uniform and the ox's ass kept time on the backbeat. His wife was yammering, something about never even looking into her eyes. Joe, she said, are you listening to me?

Going to show me Dago, he said.

You don't look in my eyes, either, she said.

Joe was awake at midnight, on his side, facing away from Mary. He was awake two hours later when he heard a car pull up and the front door open and close. Joe crept downstairs. His son had placed the couch cushions on the floor and unrolled a smelly sleeping bag. Why the hell don't you sleep in your own bed? Joe asked.

Paulie said he didn't want to wake up Angelo and besides, he was used to the bag. He reeked of cigarette smoke and booze. Joe watched him slide out of his pants and into the musty bag. His legs were thin and pimply, and even the boy's underwear was olive-drab

colored. Joe sat on the couch frame and cleared his throat. Your
mother and I want to know your plans, he said.

Day after tomorrow, Paulie said. He yawned luxuriously. We fly
south out of Travis. Lay on the beach. These guys saved my fucking
life, Dad.

Could you watch your goddamned language? Joe asked.

Sorry. I'm bushed, Dad. I am really sorry.

Joe sat for another ten minutes wanting to say many things
which seemed stuck in his throat. His son started snoring, and Joe
hit the light switch.

He couldn't sleep. Dinner at his mother's had felt disjointed by
the conspicuous absence of the war hero, by the defensive expression on Penny's face whenever Paulie was mentioned by Ludovico
or Gino, by the whimpering of Mickey and the recounting of the
Santa Claus story. Joe's brother Narciso was particularly agitated by
Saint Nick's poor treatment of little Mickey, who weighed in at a
good fifty pounds more than Narciso himself. Mary had drunk too
much and said too much, Penny had said something snide about the
government, and Angelo had taken that opportunity to do his im-
personation of President Johnson's Texas twang: Let us all ree-zin
to-gay-ther, mah fellah Amer-kins.

There was a phone in the basement, and Joe wrapped himself in
a towel and started to dial Julie's number, then decided she might
hate him for it at this ungodly hour, and not just because it would
shake her from a deep sleep but also because it would show a weakness of his character. He went back to the kitchen and poured himself a glass of brandy, then climbed back into his marriage bed.

A few hours later Joe was back in the basement with a cup of instant java and the towel over his shoulders. Julie sounded sleepy and soft. I needed to hear your voice, Joe told her.

They talked on for a while, and while they talked Mickey got up and padded to the kitchen in her blue Chinatown pajamas. She had a phone number for the North Pole which the paper had published last week, but when she picked up the kitchen phone she heard her father's voice. He sounded strange. A woman's voice was there, too, and they said things to each other about weird things, about how she wished he could get his shit together, about how he wished he could hold her on his lap. Mickey thought of sitting on Santa's lap and saying what you wished for, and she said, Daddy, why are you wishing for that? and then the phone went dead. She listened to the silent chamber of the phone and tried to dial Santa's workshop at the North Pole, then set the phone down. She walked into the living room where the sleeping bag with her brother in it filled most of the space and leaned over Paulie to ask him to help with the phone.

In an instant her head was slammed onto the carpet. Both of her arms were twisted behind her back, and several places in her body were in pain, but the wind was knocked out of her stomach so her mouth couldn't scream.

A moment later her brother released her. He knelt beside her and said, Oh, Mickey, fuck me, man, goddamn it, I am so fucking sorry.

And her father was there an instant later, kneeling beside them on the floor as she started bawling, and then her mother and other brother and baby sister stampeding down the stairs like horses while Paulie leaned against the couch frame in his green underwear and muttered curse words at his own feet.

They took Mickey to the doctor, and her mother said she'd fallen off the garage roof, and the doctor said her shoulder was dislocated. Paulie was gone by the time they returned, and so was her dad, and she wondered about the telephone and the line to call to make a wish, and why her father had been wishing with some woman, but the doctor's pills made her so sleepy she stopped wondering, and about the time she took her coat off she was falling asleep.

She could hear her sister when she woke up. Her sister Penny was talking with her mother about Paulie, and Mickey thought then that she should live with Penny from now on, in an apartment near the college in San Francisco, so she'd be safe from Paulie.

They were standing outside her door, Mom and Penny talking about Paulie. Her mom sounded kind of mad at Penny, and then her brother started arguing with Penny, like her mom had left and the boy had jumped in like a tag-team wrestler to take her place. You know, Angelo said, Mickey looked just about like one of them.

One of them? One of whom, Penny asked in a hard voice.

Pardon my French, Angie said, but to Paulie she would look like a gook.

Jesus, Penny said, please don't add racism to your mountainous ignorance.

Well, I mean, she was wearing those pajamas, and she has those Oriental eyes.

This justifies our brother attacking our sister?

Well, they say you should never sneak up on a soldier, especially when he's asleep. I read that somewhere. I think that was one of my Sergeant Rock comics, Angelo said.

I'd be the last person on Earth to contradict Sergeant Rock, Penny said, but I think there's something sick going on in our country when your brother practically kills your sister by mistake just because his mind is so screwed up by this fucking war.

Hey, Angelo said, somebody has to fight.

No they don't, Penny said. Paulie wasn't even drafted, and he re-upped last year. He's sick, you guys. He's General Westmoreland's little robot.

And you're Ho Chi Minh's, Angelo said.

She could feel it, the lines being drawn, and Mickey knew she and Penny were on the same side. Maybe they were both more Oriental than the others or something. Smaller, feminine, weaker. The papers and the TV showed them now and then, the little Chinese-looking people getting killed by the American soldiers like Paulie, and the little people were supposed to be bad, they were Reds, but she could tell her sister was on their side, and so was she because she and Penny were more like them than the American soldiers.

But she still loved Paulie, and it was so scary to think that her brother could be changed into something mean by Satan. She and Penny went out for lunch later that day in Berkeley, they wore the same sweatshirts and jeans like they were twins except Mickey had to wear a sling, and they had Chinese noodles because they both liked Oriental things. In fact, Penny bought her a beaded necklace from an import store and a fat little Buddha you could rub the belly on for good luck, and they walked among the Christmas lights of downtown, and Penny stuck her middle finger out at the Hink's store.

After Penny left for her apartment Mickey lay on her bed and thought about Paulie slamming her face down and wrenching her arms, and she started crying again. Her mom tried to cheer her up, and Uncle Ciso came by with a box of chocolates, but she kept crying. Paulie's attack was mixed up in her mind with the strange things her father and that woman had been wishing for on the phone, as if a kind of craziness had come into her house over the telephone wires and made her brother and father act like different people. And the woman seemed like she was from far away, maybe even the North Pole, and maybe her father wanted things he could never have, and Mickey drifted into sleep and dreams and wondered if she were still dreaming when, several hours later, she heard her parents talking through the wall next to her bed.

Her father said he was not happy here, and her mother said who is, but her father said, no, he meant here, in this house, and her mom was quiet for a minute. Then she started crying, and her father said, Mary, and she said there was a woman, and he said there wasn't a woman but he was just unhappy, and Mickey thought of the woman from the North Pole that her father wanted to hold on his lap. She heard them hiss at each other like snakes through the wall, and then the sound of doors opening and closing and the car starting up and leaving. Mickey cried into her pillow and her mom came to her bedroom and they cried together and fell asleep.

The weekend before Christmas Mickey's uncles went to Reno, and Narciso complained about what was breaking his poor niece's heart to anybody who would listen. One sympathetic ear was attached to one of the ugliest faces in the casino, the massive and brutally scarred countenance of James Scalabini, who was known by his associates as Jimmy the Finger. What kind of bastard, Jimmy wanted to know, breaks the heart of a little retarded girl?

It was the night before Christmas, and Paulie Verbicaro lay asleep on the concrete floor of a noisy hotel in Ensenada. His father lay alone in a motel room in Oakland with a sprained lower back, brooding about his son and his wife and Julie, occasionally picking up and setting down the telephone, eventually taking a sleeping pill and saying *sayonara* to the whole damned holiday. Penny sat in the kitchen with her mother and helped her drink a bottle of chianti, imagining it her job to help the younger children understand that their parents were fighting, that their father had just needed to get away and be by himself for a few days. This wasn't the first time they'd fought or the first time he'd taken off, though, and her brother Angelo, who was upstairs singing in a terrible voice, and her baby sister, who was laughing at the TV, didn't seem particularly upset.

Mickey was upset, though. She sat by the window, as she had done every Christmas Eve, and stared into the sky through tears.

Even though her brother had told her that Santa was just a story and that the guy at Hink's was probably just a bum, she kept her eyes on the stars.

She remembered that Christmas was about Jesus, and not just Santa, and she thought it might be a sin to wish so much for presents on Jesus's birthday, so she started saying, Happy Birthday, Jesus. Happy Birthday, Jesus, she said, over and over. Suddenly Lady-Bird started yelping.

And what to Mickey's eyes should appear but Santa himself being led from a taxi to her front door by the biggest and ugliest man she'd ever seen. Merry Christmas, Mickey, the huge man said. You are Mickey, ain't youse? She picked up Lady-Bird and nodded. The man was grinning, and his teeth looked yellow and pointed. Look who's here. I brung him all the way from the North Pole.

Three of Santa's ribs and one of his thumbs were broken, but the fat man managed a jolly ho-ho-ho and allowed the giant to escort him to a chair. Santa said he wanted to personally apologize to Mickey and her family and make sure he heard the child's wish for Christmas.

Hey, Santa said to Mary and Penny, wincing as he eased into the chair, I was completely out of line with the girl and her father. Completely.

Mickey's mother and older sister stood in the living room with mouths open and wineglasses held under their chins as if to catch their teeth in them. Her baby sissy, Janine, clutched her mom's dress. A new Beatles album which Angelo had found and opened early was playing a song called No Reply from the upstairs, but the boy was downstairs now, too.

Everybody makes a mistake, Jimmy the Finger said. He winked, then urged Mickey to sit on Santa's lap. The fat man's face went white at the suggestion, and he made a sound like a balloon letting out some air when she sat on him, but he managed to ask her what she wanted for Christmas.

Well, Mickey said, do you have enough time to make this stuff on Christmas Eve?

No problem, Santa squealed. But if you could please sit still.

I got a long list, Mickey said.

He don't care, Jimmy the Finger said. Them reindeer ain't going nowhere.

How come you came in a taxi and not a sled?

He's saving his reindeer for later on tonight, the huge man said. Go ahead and ask him for anything you want. Especially things from Hink's.

Mickey shifted her weight, which made the jolly fellow squeal like Lady-Bird did when Mickey hugged her too hard. Oh, my God, her brother Angelo said. Mom, I just realized that *Santa* and *Satan* are the same name with one letter moved. Did you ever think of that, Mom?

Angelo, don't get started.

Seriously, that's gotta mean something, Angelo said.

Mickey, Santa's busy, her mom said. Her face was white as Santa's beard, her voice trembling. Tell him what you want so he can get going.

Janine clutched her mother's dress like a mountaineer on a cliff. That's not Santa Claus, she whispered.

There were so many things Mickey wanted, but for some reason it was hard to wish. Part of her was thrilled by Santa's visit, by the prospect of having her every dream come true, but another part of her knew that Santa looked kind of pathetic and couldn't really bring her happiness right now. She knew there was some sickness going around the whole country, like her sister had said. Her brother Paulie had it, and so did her father, and probably so did Santa and his big assistant in the checkered sport coat. She got up.

Hey, kid, Santa said, what do you want?

Angelo once told her that for Santa to actually fly to every house in the world and bring a gift to every person like a magical astronaut orbiting the planet he'd need to move faster than Superman. She went to her room and returned with the figurine of the Buddha.

Here, she said. He has a big belly like you.

Santa stood slowly and accepted the gift. You're a nice kid, he said. His eyes were moist. You're a very nice kid.

Ain't that nice, Jimmy the Finger said. Hey, where's the johnny? He lumbered down the hall.

Rub the belly, Santa, Mickey said as she showed him to the door. She kissed his cheek. You better skedaddle.

She smiled and waved as Santa, with the Buddha still clutched in his gloved hand, hopped down the steps. He ran faster than you'd think a fat man could, making a beeline for his sleigh and the houses of all the children in the world, disappearing into the night.

CIGARS

Ludovico

Ludovico Verbicaro loved a good cigar and the idea of its leaves harvested by brown-skinned women on a tropical island where the mountains disappeared in steaming clouds. He loved a good scrap ending with a knockout, a ball smacked out of the park, a tee shot over the drink and fifty yards past the young guys a foot taller than himself. Lu loved the little guys from the Caribbean who played their nuts off and slid on their bellies under the catcher's glove, the underdogs with the huge heart, the rally in the bottom of the ninth. He lived for these moments, but he nearly died for them, too, over and over, his own heart and his stomach and some place in the back of his brain nearly snapped in two when they happened. While his handsome, dim-witted older brother drifted along with a smile and a winning ticket, and his younger brother calculated and schemed the smartest course to take, Lu followed his heart and his gut and that place on his brain stem which often seemed about to snap like a suspender strap, and he rode his number out to the bitter end.

In the summer of 1970 Lu was riding a long shot that could put him in cigars and bananas for the rest of his life or, more likely, could land him in prison and lifelong debt. He'd already run up a debt from gambling which a year of his salary from the family business couldn't cover, and he kept this a secret from the brothers he shared the construction business with. He owed six hundred dollars in parking and traffic tickets alone, and his Chrysler Imperial needed a transmission he couldn't afford, so he told his family he was tired of driving. He put another mortgage on the house he rarely spent time in since his children had grown up and his wife had passed away, and he threw ten grand he didn't have into a scheme orchestrated by a little wise guy named Jimmy Olivera.

How Lu met Jimmy began with a conversation in the late '50s with Jimmy's brother-in-law, a made man from the East Coast whom Lu happened to meet at the dog races. The man said he was part of the Gambino family of New Jersey, and that he had come to the Bay Area to make a few investments with his associates. Lu and his older brother, Narciso, welcomed their interest because they seemed like great guys with a lot of money to spare, but their younger brother, Joe, turned the Jersey men down a few days later. No hard feelings and no disrespect intended, but Joe said they had a small business and all they could do to keep it small enough to manage and keep Uncle off their backs. Lu could hardly believe his brother's balls at saying this to New Jersey, but the leader of the entourage said he understood.

A dozen years later this same man, jowly and white-haired now, had another business proposition for the Verbicaro brothers, and Joe did his best to turn him down again. The man stared across the table a moment, his cheeks coloring. A man comes to you in good faith to ask a favor, for which he will gladly pay you very well. Joe swallowed and nodded. A brother-in-law, the man said, a nice guy with not much talent or initiative, to be honest, needs some office space here in California for a small import business.

Hell, he can have Ciso's desk, Lu said. Narciso nodded.

Office and a little storage space is all he needs, the mafioso murmured. He waved a hand to a young man who'd sat silently at the table through all five courses of lunch, and the young man opened a briefcase and placed some papers on the table next to the calamari. Lu reached for the papers, and Joe put his hand on his arm.

Hold the phone, Amos, Joe said, trying to sound like Andy in the old radio program.

What's the problem now, Mr. Verbicaro?

Yeah? Lu wanted to know.

Joe squinted at the contract, but he wasn't reading it, he was averting his eyes and buying time to cool off and think. Office and storage space, Joe said, as if he were studying the paper. Hmm. Joe was remembering the conversation he'd had with his brothers right after their first meeting with these Jersey guys, how Lu and Ciso had finally seemed to grasp the significance of steering clear of mobsters, how even their mother had scolded them for being so naive. The black hand, their old mother had said, I knew who those boys were in the old country. They're all a bunch of lost ducks.

What the hell does Ciso use his desk for? Lu asked. He puts golf tees in the drawers.

I got a lot of addresses in there, Ciso said. People I know. But, hell, I could share it.

Joe cleared his throat and told New Jersey he'd lease them half of one of his two old warehouses, which he really never filled now that business was slow, and erect a partition and office in it for the brother-in-law and his business. Power, utilities, maintenance of street access, all part of the lease agreement. I'll write it up, have your man here look it over, and we all sign. Totally separate businesses.

Why do you worry so much about keeping things separate?

Something our old man taught me. What does this guy import?

The mafioso grimaced and stared into Joe's eyes a moment, then he smiled. He sighed. My little sister's husband, Jimmy. He tries, you know? He's a little soft up here. He tapped his forehead, and both Joe and Lu nodded, and the three men glanced at Narciso and nodded some more. He tries. He brings in coffee, Italian cheeses, cigars. That kind of thing.

Cigars? Hell, he can have my desk, Lu said, and all the men, save Joe, chuckled.

A year later, the brother-in-law's office remained dark twenty-two hours out of twenty-four. The door had no business title or name painted on it, and the storage space usually held a few cardboard boxes connected by hammocks of spiderweb, and a few salamis and cheeses hanging in a corner above a couple of oil drums. Whenever the door was open, Ciso and Lu would stop, and

Jimmy Olivera would give them cigars and whatever he had around that month, some chianti, a little sheep's cheese. This new stuff was always right there in the little office space, in the file cabinet or on the desk. The desk was Ciso's, and most of the furniture had come from the brothers, including a phone which Lu had hooked up to their own business line. What the hell does Jimmy need a phone bill for if he's here twice a month? Lu had said, and Jimmy had thanked him heartily.

For all his connection with the wealth of the East Coast, Jimmy seemed perpetually broke. He bummed lunch and rides from the brothers. His own car, which he always parked behind the warehouse next to a Dumpster, was an old Buick Century whose paint, like Jimmy's hairline, was receding on top. His suit was nice, but he always wore the same thing, and the knees and elbows were shiny and thin. His expensive Italian shoes were over a decade old, and the shape of his big toes advertised themselves like the handprints in front of Grauman's Chinese.

Olivera could tell a good story, though, and both Lu and Ciso loved to hear him talk. He talked about huge bets he'd won, trips to the Caribbean, show-business people he'd met. He talked about that dirty son of a bitch Castro, and how the increased price of cigars was a direct effect of communism. Olivera had frequent words about Castro, about how much he'd love to be the one to put a bullet in his head.

Once in a great while, maybe three times that year to Lu's knowledge, the warehouse would go from empty to filled to the rafters overnight. It seemed that only Lu and Ciso were privy to this, and only if they happened to stumble onto Jimmy the day after delivery. Olivera told them to keep it under their hats. Timing, he said, was everything in his line, and if they were to tell people, like their brother Joe, for instance, and word got around, his prices would sink. Then some morning, maybe a week or two later, they'd drop by, and Jimmy's warehouse would be empty again, as if dwarves or mice had carried everything off in the night, and Jimmy would have some new box of chocolate or a crate of banana liquor to share with them on Ciso's bare desk.

Lu knew Jimmy wasn't soft in the head like Ciso, so he wondered why the Jersey guys had seemed so hesitant about him. Lu's own brothers-in-law, his sisters' husbands, were slow workers and hard drinkers who put in their days and anesthetized themselves every evening with Jack Daniels. Olivera, to Lu, was maybe more of a dreamer, more of a gambler and schemer, and for this Lu found him lovable.

It takes a dreamer to make something big happen, and it takes a risk, and this was where Lu's ten thousand dollars came in. One spring morning they drove past the warehouse, and the office door was ajar, and Lu could see the glowing tip of a stogie in the shadows. Soon they were talking, and Olivera asked them if they wanted to go in on something big, something humongous, a once-in-a-lifetime deal. Ciso said, No, thanks, and fooled with the radio dial, but Lu asked Olivera to elaborate. The little guy's eyes darted at Ciso, and Lu sent Ciso to the local market for some orange juice and batteries, and the two dreamers leaned over the desk after he'd gone. It had to do with cigars, the very best cigars in the world, the best crop they'd get for a decade or maybe forever because Jimmy knew a few things most people didn't. Like how they'd had their bumper crop in Cuba this year, and how a few guys who worked for Sam Trafficante were thinking it was time to kick Castro in the balls and fix international prices by dropping some napalm on some tobacco farms, and how he could get things past the customs guys, etc., etc. Right now even, you know how much I could get for this torpedo I'm smoking if I was to sell it in Switzerland?

Lu said he had no idea, but he guessed as high as three bucks. Olivera said more.

More than three bucks? You fishin' me? Okay, four-fifty.

Try fifteen, Olivera said.

Lu was a dreamer and a gambler with physical talents, a small, compact guy, barrel-chested but not muscle-bound, light on his feet even in his fifties. A Coast League third-sacker in his youth, a smooth dancer and loud laugher at a party, and the only one in his family of house builders who knew how to lay a foundation and raise a roof, Lu learned everything with his whole body, with his legs and arms moving. He'd cleared lots with his brothers and his old man, jumped freights during the Depression to pick hops and grapes in Napa, cut steel in a mill in Emeryville until the racket nearly ruined his ears. During the war, when housing was in demand, he cut and pounded planks and told the crew of *paisanos* what to do while his little brother, Joe, made the bids and the deals. Business talk from Joe at lunch flew over his head or made him close his eyes and think of music or women or thoroughbreds, so he'd usually change the subject as quickly as he could, before he fell asleep in his bowl of minestrone. Just take me to the goddamn site and let me figure it out, he'd tell Joe, and Joe would sigh and raise his eyebrows.

Lu's wife, Hen, succumbed to cancer when she and Lu were fifty, and Lu fell into a three-year drinking and gambling project which his daughter helped him overcome. She screamed at him for half an hour and tossed a dozen bottles out the window, including orange juice. One dead parent is enough, she said, and Lu said *sayonara* to the booze.

By his late fifties, after decades of crew-bossing and job-dispatching, Lu was barely needed at the family business, and the business had changed so much that he barely identified with it. They worked small pieces of huge tract-house deals, they used staples and pressboard instead of nails and wood, used preformed, precut, precast crap, and there were so many goddamned regulations you needed Perry Mason before you made a decision. Also, they barely stayed afloat, even with Joe running things, because of the big guys in the industry. Lu felt like he was way out in left field most of the time, so he and his older brother, Narciso, got breakfast, read the papers, checked into the office with Joe and Sammy, the book-keeper, looked things over, found out what their kids were up to that day (their sons drove trucks and forklifts), gabbed with Olivera, and, often as not, took off for the horses or a ballgame with him. Unofficially, they were considered the company's trouble-shooters, which meant that when things were going haywire, if

some outfit didn't deliver the goods or someone was drinking on
the job, Joe told his brothers and they took off in Ciso's Cadillac to
take care of the problem, but officially they were nonworking
shareholders.

So it might be that Lu, his stomach on fire with Olivera's cigar
scheme and his recent investment, may have been unconsciously
gathering players for the wise guy's game when he did his trou-
bleshooting that morning. He asked his older brother: Okay, this
son of a bitch, Sinclair, staggering around piss-drunk on that Hay-
ward job—you know what he looks like?

The Cadillac with the two nattily dressed middle-aged Italian
guys pulled up next to the canteen truck at the construction site.
Ciso, you hear what I'm saying? You know this Sinclair?

Lu, that's Jennifer with the truck. Narciso stepped out of the
car and began talking with the pretty girl at the canteen. Lu could
see him rocking back on his heels, laughing at something the girl
had said. The big flirt with an angel for a wife and one flashlight bat-
tery for a brain. Lu got out, adjusted his tie, yanked on the pleat in
his trousers, massaged his neck. The truck and Caddy were on
packed clay near some tar tubs and a smelly outhouse. Lu found
Pete Russo, the foreman for one of the big boys, who pointed in
Sinclair's direction. One of them *colored* guys your brother hired,
Russo said with a smirk. The wind blew Lu's tie over his shoulder
like a scarf. He whistled for Narciso to follow him.

The site was vast: skeletal tracts on landfill like a disaster scene,
acres of roofless frames where families and furniture might have
been swept out by a tornado. A whiff of bay stink mingled with ce-

ment dust, plaster, and the occasional smell of turds from the simple wooden privy. Lu and Ciso made a beeline for the two men Russo had pointed out.

Sinclair saw them. Those two old wop dagos give me any shit, I'll knock their greasy heads together, he told the old guy, Walker, who knelt beside him and loaded a staple gun.

Huh, Walker said. The response meant something to Sinclair which didn't help the young man's confidence. The Verbicaro brothers were close now, the one strutting like a bantam rooster, the other trying to keep from spilling the contents of two Styrofoam cups.

Which one of you guys is Sinclair? Lu asked as he approached.

You're lookin' at him. Sinclair belched and wobbled slightly in his work boots.

Give me a damned good reason why I shouldn't can your ass right now.

You guys want some hot chocolate? Ciso asked.

What? Sinclair stared at Narciso.

Hey, the man just asked you something.

Naw, I don't drink that.

That what you say to somebody, Sinclair, they offer you something?

You want some, Lu?

Lu shot Ciso a murderous glance. Nobody never taught you how to talk to somebody, Sinclair? Maybe show somebody good manners?

No, *thanks,* I mean. Sinclair shook his head, clenched and unclenched his fists. His hard hat swayed back and forth on the crown of his Afro. You satisfied?

What kind of crap *do* you drink, Sinclair? Smells like beer.

I don't drink on the job.

Oh, hey, I never mentioned drinkin' on the job, did I, Ciso?

Jennifer sold me these, Lu. Here. Ciso set the chocolates next to Walker, who laid the staple gun down and thanked him.

Did I mention drinkin' on the job? Lu addressed this question first to his brother, who was tying a shoe, then to Walker. Walker chuckled and shook his head. He stood now, a head taller than Lu.

Young bucks, Walker said. He chuckled again. Ain't you Lu Verbicaro? Played third base for the Missions?

Lu gave the man his hand.

Jimmy Walker. We tussled a few times.

Jimmy Walker. Wait. Son of a bitch! Jimmy Walker?

That's right.

Ciso, this guy is Jimmy Walker!

Who's that? Ciso brushed cement dust from his trouser cuffs.

Jimmy Walker. It just hit me because I seen that name in the books last week. Who's *that*, Ciso? You and Joe don't know you hired the best goddamned pitcher in California?

You guys play on the same team? Ciso asked, still working on his cuffs.

Lu rolled his eyes. A hundred years of Jim Crow could pass under his brother's nose unnoticed. Hell, Ciso, he had to play in the Negro Leagues. Used to play us exhibition and beat us every goddamned time. This guy struck out the DiMaggio brothers, for Christ sake.

Vince DiMaggio, Ciso said, as if reciting prayers over the rosary beads. Dominick DiMaggio. Joe DiMaggio.

Negro Leagues, Sinclair said. He sniggered.

Lu and Walker sat on a stack of Sheetrock and smoked cigars. Cubans he'd gotten from Olivera, Cohibas with their rich coffee bite and chocolate sweetness, with a spicy tickle on your tongue that made you think of dark women with mischievous smiles. While Lu and Jimmy talked baseball, Ciso yakked with Jennifer and helped the girl close the truck to head for another work site. Then he climbed into his Cadillac and took off.

Sinclair watched the old guys smoke their stogies, cursed under his breath, then went back to work. Since it was a hot day he finished most of the six-pack of Colt 45 malt liquor before lunch. He sang a James Brown song as he carried scraps of Sheetrock and shingles and tossed them into a gigantic Dumpster, and he staggered and almost fell a couple of times. The other men, most of them Teamsters and old rednecks who worked for a big corporation, gave the young man a wide berth or laughed and shook their heads at him. Like a dull knife, just ain't cuttin', Sinclair sang, you talkin' aloud, but ain't sayin' nuttin'.

They were talking about Juan Maricial's delivery, his sky-kick and windmill motion, when Pete came by to tell Lu that Sinclair was drunk again, and that Ciso had driven off, some time ago, without him. Walker was poker-faced at the news of Sinclair's drinking. Of course Lu could smell the liquor on Walker's breath, but he didn't know what to do with the information. Lu could hear the singing above the racket of air compressors. It sounded at times like the young man was shouting at somebody. Talkin' aloud! Huh! Ain't sayin' nuttin'! Ain't sayin' nuttin'!

An hour later the idea hit Lu between the eyes, and he started to lay it across the table to his little brother, Joe, at the Topsy-Turvy before he knew what he was about. Joe was preoccupied with a hot pastrami and the details of a contract he was about to sign with a group of plasterers and lathers and didn't really listen to Lu until he heard his own son's name mentioned. Joe's son was a heroin addict, recently, and dishonorably, discharged from the U.S. Marine Corps. Lu knew that dreamers take risks. Joe's son Paulie was what he'd call a dreamer. He knew that dreamers made mistakes, sometimes very big mistakes, and that was what family was for, to help each other out after we make our mistakes, not to act like you can't talk to your own kid because things are too screwed up. That was why Jimmy Walker was picking up the beer cans behind his punk nephew, and that was why Lu told Joe that they should find Paulie at that fleabag hotel in San Francisco and force him to work. Somebody had to do it.

What's this about Paulie? Joe squinted as if in bright light.

What made me think of it was that nephew of Jimmy Walker's.

Jimmy who?

Jesus Christ, Joe, you don't know who you hired last month, do you?

Walker, the older black guy, I got no problem with him, Lu. It was the young guy, Sinclair.

Jimmy Walker?

Johnny Sinclair.

Jimmy Walker? Retires the side nine innings in a row, exhibition?
I don't get you.

Augie Gallan turns to me and says he'd rather face Bobby
Feller? Jimmy Walker?

Joe's jaw dropped, and a sliver of marbled beef fell onto his
chin. You gotta be kiddin' me. Why the hell is he workin' for a two-
bit joint like us?

Laid off, somewhere in Emeryville.

Christ, Lu, he was probably forty when you played him thirty
years ago. You sure that's Jimmy Walker?

The great ones, Joe. I've seen it. They disappear and nobody
gives a flying shit about them anymore. I've seen it.

Lu waited until he was back in Joe's Lincoln Continental before
he returned to his plan. I got an idea, Joe. You listening to me?

Ciso just took off on you again? Joe laughed. You better get that
Imperial running.

It happens. Hey, Joe, I got an idea for Paulie.

Joe nosed the luxury sedan onto the freeway and scowled.

You listening to me, Joe?

Joe's son, Paulie, had returned from Vietnam angry and addicted to heroin, and he was now living among derelicts in a hotel
south of Market. All Joe knew was that Paulie took something
called methadone every day and refused any help or communication
from his father.

What about him?

Lu's idea was to have Paulie work alongside Jimmy Walker and Jimmy's nephew Sinclair.

Nephew?

The kid is a drunk which, excuse me for sayin' it, but I gotta call a spade a spade here, Joe, which is not half as bad as your son.

You want my son to work with a drunk?

The kid is like all sorts of them kids now, Joe, he thinks he's a Black Panther or whatever the hell it is. But I say you let a man like Jimmy Walker supervise the two of them, and you'll see some results. Get your boy off his ass over there in Frisco. It's time for him to move on.

Lu was right that his nephew needed to be forced to move, and that he'd been so injured by the events of recent years that he had forgotten how. Maybe Lu's dreaming included Paulie in the way men so often include others without consulting them. Maybe Lu and Ciso were able to imagine coercing their nephew into productivity in a way the young man's parents weren't.

Lu knew that there is a time in a young man's life when the entire world is spread before him, and to play ball and follow a dream, or to slip an arm around a pretty girl's waist and laugh, seems a birthright. That time had come and gone too quickly for Paulie Verbicaro. He'd done something embarrassing in his seventeenth year, he had caused a local scandal and then left home, and the armed forces, and the Saigon whores who were really little girls or painted crones, and the daily fear that ran through his viscera had erased that hopeful hour of youth.

Paulie had come home dishonorably discharged, a junkie with little meat on his bones, fewer thoughts in his head, and even less hope in his heart, and now he was a methadone addict on skid row. His clothes, even his bushy hair and beard, were stiff with sweat and filled with tobacco and weed and beer stink. He imagined that his rankness and filth and ideas had about them an air of honesty, a piece of the truth which the suits and ties on Market and the neat college kids playing flower child in their bare feet and cut-off jeans knew nothing about. What it was about had nothing to do with peace and justice or communism or Nixon or all the other bullshit people spoke about. What it was about was death.

People you love die. Babies and mothers die. People who never smoked or ate a Big Mac, like his Aunt Min, keel over with cancer. Some nice kid maybe steps out into the street to grab her kitty and a fucking Toys "R" Us truck whacks her. There is no reason or plan behind it, except that life, or God Himself, is full of some cold shit, and that was about all that Paulie knew.

His mother, his father, his sisters and brother, even a couple of old high school friends had come to see him a few times, delivered food or money to his room south of Market, but he knew he scared them off fast. A couple of druggy women were interested in him, probably the kind who need to care for the wounded, undoubtedly wounded themselves, fat earth mothers on acid, drunks and pot-heads who found something intriguing in a full-out junkie, or even a few who were drawn to a man who'd killed, that weird breed of woman who hangs around prisons and barracks smelling the blood, probably girls of mean-ass fathers with a killer's gleam in their eyes who withheld the love these girls had always craved. Paulie didn't know, but he needed a woman now and then, that soft creaminess of a woman's skin, so he prowled at least once a week for a woman's touch like a dog with an empty belly, but the only one he'd been in love with was unknown to his family, and she'd killed herself last spring in Saigon.

May was half Asian and half French, and he wasn't even sure how you spelled her name, but it was pronounced Gway May, and she was about thirty-five and had three kids. He met her at the pharmacy where she sold mostly penicillin to GIs with the clap, and they started sleeping together soon after, and he started proposing marriage days after that. Almond eyes and freckles, auburn hair, and a nose somewhere between the steeples along the Loire and the round huts along the Mekong, and all they could do was make love and hazard words for the things around them in French and English and Vietnamese. He would spend six months out in hell and then a month in her fishy apartment among the kids and the grouchy grandmother, naming things as if they were newly formed on the earth, and clinging as if their bodies might fly away in the night. From what he gathered she'd overdosed on barbiturates and rum about three days before his return from a tour. Always sad, the toothless grandmother told him, Gway May always sad.

Heroin had seemed the only honest thing since. How could he explain? There was no logic about it. Heroin made him aware of something which had to do with *being,* which had something to do with May still *being.* Whenever Paulie tried to put it into words people shook their heads or, if they were stoned, nodded stupidly without understanding, and he knew he sounded just as stupid talking about it. Methadone made him feel permanently stupid and spaced out and kind of mellow, and it kept him from shooting up because the government knew and he knew that if he shot enough smack to get off now he'd kill himself. Methadone kept him out of the junk market, and only combined with a couple of joints and a quart of pale ale did it come close to good.

Once a day Paulie stood in line for a cup of orange juice with his narcotic in it. They always gave him a donut and coffee, too. Once a month he stood in line for money from the government which required some blood work and proof of his daily orange juice, as well as a pep talk about how a slowly decreasing dosage would make him clean and ready for work. He always tried to picture himself working, maybe selling tickets at a porno theater, something that took no brains or physical stamina. Paulie had been a talented athlete in high school, but now it took a singular effort to walk to the county office, especially after a couple of joints or a quart of Rainier. He had to climb two hills to get there, and sometimes on the way back he'd buy lunch at this noodle house in Chinatown and stretch out with a quart afterward in that Chinese park where the old men played mah-jongg and the pigeons landed on his paper bag or his foot, and he'd get the best sleep of the month, even if a couple of pigeons pecked and shat on him, right there in the park.

He was thinking about the girl behind the counter, the way her kneecaps looked so flat and small when she knelt to get something, when he fell asleep in the park in Chinatown. In the dream she reached across the counter to touch his cheek, and soon they were kissing. Full of curried noodle soup and beer and Uncle Sam's controlled opiate, Paulie drifted under this girl's dress until a soft hiccupping came to his ear. Somebody was right next to him, practically on top of him. It took Paulie a while to acknowledge this because part of his mind felt too good to let go of the dream while another part was accustomed to the vigilance of war. A face was hiccupping an inch from Paulie's ear, and a hand was in Paulie's front pocket, pressed right against his penis. Moving, in fact. Paulie cleared his throat, and the hand stopped moving.

Paulster, you let me explain 'fore you kill me? *Hiccup.*

It was Roger the Lodger, that weird little speed freak who panhandled and stole and begged for a place to crash free in every room in the hotel, including Paulie's. Paulie was so body-heavy tired he couldn't move. Get your hand off my dick, Roger, he managed to say.

It's stuck, man.

Stuck?

Promise you won't kill me.

Promise. Stuck?

I thought your thing was the bankroll.

What?

I thought your thing was money, you understand what I'm sayin'? Then you roll on your belly and I got stuck.

Roger was a small, wild-haired, white gnome of indeterminate age who sometimes sounded like a streetwise black kid from Hunter's Point and other times sounded like Grandpappy Amos from *The Real McCoys*. I'm sorry, Paulster, I didn't plan to rob you, I come to warn you, man. He hiccupped again. Roll over, man, these Chinamen lookin' at us like we really strange.

We are really strange, Paulie said. His body was so tired he didn't know if he was able to roll over yet. His legs felt like wooden posts attached to a concrete torso, at the nexus of which throbbed one piece of flesh with Roger's hand under it. His beard was damp from his own drool. Were you jacking me off, Lodger?

Oh, man. *Hiccup.* I kind of, I don't know. Thinkin' if I help you make it to the mountaintop, then when you step over into the promised land there be enough room to get my hand out, you understand? *Hiccup.* Not my preference for the entire situation, but I was tryin' to make the best of a bad deal. Hey, I'm still stuck, you got to move.

Paulie managed to turn his pelvis enough to free Roger's hand. What's this bullshit about warning me?

There's some mafia out to get you, and I swear to God, on my mother's Bible, man, that is the God's fucking truth.

You didn't come to rob me because it's the day I get a check from Uncle?

You think I pay attention on your schedule with Uncle Sam? Roger shook his little hand like a rag at the end of his arm and massaged his elbow with the other. I come to warn you, man, I reckon because I care for you. Then when I find you I thought maybe to seize an opportunity, you understand what I'm sayin', maybe a dollar or two, but you gonna thank me you didn't walk in on those bad motherfuckers. You owe them some money or something?

Paulie thought about this as he watched Roger pace back and forth and shake his sore hand like a flag of surrender in front of the dignified older men who sat holding tile dominoes at the little tables. Did he still owe money to that guy, Lenny, who'd sold him a few lids of dope last winter? Lenny had a scar like a shiny eraser mark across his nose and cheek where some goons had poured acid as a kind of late-payment fee. Had Lenny fingered him for some reason?

I was you, Roger said, still massaging his arm, I'd keep clear that hotel. Hey, Paulster, could you loan me a couple of bucks? Where you keep it, in your boots?

The third time that day the Cadillac parked in front of the hotel the Lodger saw them and nearly peed his pants running up the stairs to warn Paulie. He found him in bed with Janey. It was late afternoon, and the fog had come and gone, letting jagged lines of light fall across the empty bottles and roach-filled ashtrays from a broken Venetian blind. Roger stared at the obese woman's exposed breast, which was larger than his head and had a stripe of light crossing its nipple, and decided to touch it by way of shaking her awake. Janey sighed. Roger hesitated. Maybe those old Cosa Nostras are looking for somebody else, he thought as he squeezed Janey like a rugby ball, but she smacked his hand and started cussing. Paulie snorted, lifted his head, and slept on, and Roger gasped about the mafia while Janey cussed him. Rapid footfalls, jingling pocket change, and a few whistled notes of Barbra Streisand echoed from the stairway. A strange harmony, two men whistling contrapuntally in the sonorous stairwell: *People, people who need people, are the luckiest people in the world.* Both Janey and Roger fled, the obese woman wriggling into her kimono as she made her way down the hall, but Paulie merely lifted his head again and fell back into a stupor until his uncles dragged him out of bed.

The brothers ate breakfast with their little brother and discussed the business and how Paulie was doing under Walker's supervision. Joe and Paulie hadn't spoken much since the dishonorable discharge, and although Joe had made several efforts, including a couple of lunches with his son during the work week, he couldn't connect with the boy's negativity, he said. He and Sinclair both seemed like the most negative people at their youthful age that Joe could imagine, always angry and sloppy and shaggy, never making eye contact, smelling of smoke and sweat and sour beer. Lu said Paulie was making progress, putting on some muscle again, and for that Joe was grateful.

Paulie discovered another honest thing that week of cold turkey, besides his own poor hygiene and withdrawal symptoms, and it was Johnny Sinclair's anger, his pure hatred of white people. He didn't know about all that Black Muslim, Black Power revolution crap and the other political things the guy said, but the hatred was something Paulie could recognize. They were shoveling gravel onto

a conveyor belt in a concrete hole somewhere south of hell or Fruit-
vale while the old guy, Walker, threw load after load into the hop-
per with a tractor of some kind. It was maybe 95 in the shade.
Paulie's strength was slowly coming back to his arms after a blur of
days of staggering and vomiting and collapsing with brooms and
shovels in his hands and getting picked up and handed a canteen by
his uncles. He and Sinclair would move their bodies vigorously for
a little while, especially the first few days when Lu and Ciso were
there, as if the kid were competing with him, then drop back and
have a beer in some half-hidden spot. They never spoke about it, except to compare brands and prices, and the old guy didn't say anything because he kept a flask of brandy on him all day and worked in
stony silence between sips, sometimes finishing two fifths by the
end of the day. Paulie was outconsumed by the kid, but he added a
couple of joints into the mix, which Sinclair only accepted a few
puffs from after the fifth day. The methadone addiction ran its course.

In the mornings Sinclair and Paulie hefted the beer-filled cooler
into the back of the pickup, where Paulie would ride with his head
leaning against the lid to keep it from blowing off even as the morning joint started raising the lid of his skull. He knew that Sinclair
couldn't abide sitting in the cab next to a white guy like himself, and
their tacit agreement to ride in separate quarters made Paulie smile
for some reason. Even when the young man got hot and started
talking like he might need to kick Paulie's white ass or line up all the
white people in the Bay Area and shoot them if he didn't move out
of the way or something, it made him grin. Go ahead, Paulie said finally, kick my ass, Panther Man.

You think I won't? Sinclair asked him. He was drunk, swaying with his chest puffed out.

Right. I think you won't.

You think I'm scared of your old Vietnam baby-killer bullshit?

I think we're both fucked up and in our own movies, Paulie said. This was an idea he frequently called to mind about people's behavior, overheard at some bar in the city. And your movie is this thing about being a black revolutionary, and my movie . . . Paulie stopped talking and stared at his beer can. His movie had to do with being the only man who could rescue this beautiful woman with three little kids in a dirty apartment in Saigon. His movie was about healing her sadness, taking her distant gaze and the mystery of her other worlds, that blend of French confection and Asian serenity, that attraction he'd always had for older women who knew more life than he, and letting her beauty and the tenderness of her loving heal his horror-filled mind. Bringing her home to the States, to a safe and quiet house in the country, to a life in which they would learn new languages to speak and he could be her protector and lover. He guessed that was his movie, but he didn't explain it to Sinclair.

The beer can flew out of his hand, smacked into a pile of lumber by Sinclair's hard hat. The boy's hands were raised in fists. Paulie dipped into the martial-arts stance he'd learned in basic. You shouldn't fly off the handle like that, he said.

Fuck your white devil baby-killer ass, Sinclair said. He moved his feet quickly, aping Muhammad Ali, but he stumbled on a chunk of Sheetrock and fell. Jimmy Walker rushed over and helped the boy up, then slapped him, hard, in the face. For a few seconds the normally stoical older man yelled in his nephew's face while Paulie stood in his karate stance, watching. The boy had tears in his eyes when he resumed work.

The anniversary of Min's death found Lu moping and drinking Scotch and getting sick and breaking his bedroom wall with a fist and patching it up with Spackle and walking most of one night and sleeping most of the next day. He stopped by his eighty-six-year-old mother's place, and the frail old woman told him to stop his moping. Enough of the sad-sack look, Rosari said. No more crying in your beer.

When he got back to his routine he learned that Ciso had bought a boat from Olivera, a boxy-looking red thing with an outboard motor and a shark decal on the hull. Tipped into the grass like some prehistoric herbivore, it reclined on a trailer out in Ciso's yard next to the bathtub virgin with the Christmas lights.

The three Verbicaro brothers played nine holes before work that morning. Lu smacked two terrific tee shots but skunked all the greens. This left him with a pain in his stomach. Joe hit straight and beautifully throughout, and Ciso was out in the rough as often as the fairway, but he sank one chip shot which ricocheted off a tree and landed in the cup.

Upon their arrival at work Lu noticed Olivera's door hanging slightly ajar and the glowing tip of a cigar showing in the shadows within. Olivera waved them over. His hanky was on his neck, mopping the sweat. In the dark warehouse Lu could see dozens of steel barrels. Is this it? Lu whispered. Is this our stuff?

No, no, no, this is some other shit. We need to move this pronto, the little guy said. Think you could get the team together? Strictly on the QT?

At day's end Walker's speech was slurred, his movements slow and deliberate. He was hosing cement dust off his truck when the Cadillac pulled up. Paulie watched as the older man leaned up to the passenger door to listen to Uncle Lu. He caught his uncle's eye and came up to get a hug through the window. You boys listen to Mr. Walker here, Lu said. He's got a deal for you.

Seven hours later the young man waited for Walker and Sinclair at a donut shop on San Pablo Avenue near the flophouse he now lived in on the west end of Berkeley. Olivera and Uncle Lu opened the warehouse door but didn't turn the lights on. The men groped around for the heavy barrels, carried them to Walker's truck, and secured them with rope. It took three minutes to load, five times that to drive to some garage in a Mexican neighborhood on the south end of Oakland, where, under Olivera's supervision, they unloaded. Lu himself did more lifting than anybody else, even though the boys' combined ages were shy of his by seventeen years. They moved the cargo until the barrels were gone, and on the last trip Paulie fell asleep in the little guy's Buick while the driver bragged to Paulie's uncle about the hard labor he used to perform when he was Paulie's age. What we're doing is saving a lot of money in taxes, he said. He slapped Lu's knee and made a sharp turn which jarred

Paulie awake. Otherwise I might as well dump this shit in the bay like it was the Boston Tea Party, right? Taxation without reputation or something, right?

Right, Lu said as he massaged his neck. Something like that.

Their ship was coming in. Tuesday night, Olivera said, and it really was a ship. In fact, it would take Ciso's boat to make the catch. When Lu looked at him askance, the little guy reassured him that he'd done this kind of thing many times, down in Florida. Piece of cake. But we'll need the team, too.

Paulie and Sinclair were lying in the shade of an old cistern filled with acid wash when Lu and Ciso found them. Shovels, potato-chip bags, and crushed beer cans lay at their feet. A Bic lighter and a slim box of rolling papers rested near Paulie's stomach. The boys were shirtless, sweaty, and with their faces covered by hard hats and their jeans and torsos dusted with dry mud they looked nearly identical, the same taut musculature and sunken bellies, the same long arms and fingers. Couple of hoboes, Ciso said.

Mutt and Jeff, Lu added. I wonder where the hell Walker is?

A mixer truck pulled up to use the acid, and Lu asked the driver about Jimmy Walker and these boys. The driver had no idea. Sinclair lifted his shell at the noise of the truck and struggled to his feet, but Paulie slept on. The boy picked up a shovel and tossed some gravel into a wheelbarrow. The South Bay was in the middle of a heat wave, and new traces of sweat streaked Sinclair's back as he worked. Soon Walker's pickup appeared. The old pitcher was careful to cover a brown sack full of bottles with a sweatshirt before he went up to Lu.

Lu was surprised to hear the older man turn down his offer. I'm trying to keep this young one out of trouble, Mr. Verbicaro. Please don't think I don't appreciate it.

They sat together on the fender, a couple of old ballplayers in the dugout, chewing grass stems and spitting. Lu listened and nodded his head. That little guy. I don't mean any disrespect. I just don't want my nephew tied up in something illegal. Promised my little sister about that.

Lu pointed with his chin at the cistern and mentioned that he wanted the same for his own nephew. He told Walker that he didn't think what they were doing was seriously illegal, exactly. More like a way to beat customs taxes. Not like smuggling dope or something.

Huh, Walker said. They were silent a moment, and Lu felt foolish. That little guy, I wouldn't turn my back on him, Mr. Verbicaro. Keeps a few extra cards in his coat, I expect.

There were things you did that were a little bit illegal, Lu said, but didn't really hurt anybody. Driving too fast. Getting a tip on the horses. And he thought, but didn't say it, that it was similar to the way a man might enjoy another woman but not actually full-out cheat on his wife. He was thinking of Narciso. A little kissing and petting with some gal in a casino, maybe even a quickie some afternoon without actually taking all of your clothes off or lying in bed with a woman you didn't even particularly like or even know. He was thinking of a married woman he'd met at Harrah's Lake Tahoe.

Walker massaged the elbow of his pitching arm. His breath was rapid and ripe with fumes. Thanks, but no thanks.

The sun was falling toward the Marin Mountains, and the bay glimmered like a playground littered with bottle shards. Ciso smiled behind the wheel of the motorboat while Olivera poured champagne into paper cups, splashing the golden liquid onto his sleeve. Lu declined. He wanted to remain sharp and was reminded of his need for vigilance when Jimmy told Ciso to turn on the navigation lights and the driver sounded the Klaxon by mistake.

Paulie sat facing backward, fishing pole and champagne cup in his hands. The last joint of the day was coming on, and in the shimmering peaks of the water he saw faces, strangers who looked at him with ugly smiles. His line had no bait; it was a piece of theater devised by the little wise guy, who also wore a skipper's cap as part of the ruse. Olivera yelled over the motor's growl, some bullshit about finding pirate's treasure on an island in the Florida Keys and having to throw it overboard when the Coast Guard came to search his boat. Paulie slumped over his pole and giggled at the way his uncles ate it up. It had been a scorcher in the South Bay, but here it was much cooler. They drifted some time with the motor off, and the sky grew darker and fuzzy with a few stars and peachy clouds, and the city of San Francisco glimmered against a scarf of fog. When ships aimed their way Ciso flashed the headlight a few times as if he knew some code of the sea and laid into the Klaxon, which always made Lu jump and curse. All four of them had lines in the water now, and Olivera called out to a couple of party boats that came near, and when people asked how they were biting the little guy made up some wacky fish story, each time increasing the size of the catch.

They ate some prosciutto and sourdough and checked their watches. Once a Coast Guard or shore police boat pulled up and blinded them with their spotlight. Olivera hammed it up about fishing and asked the cops for advice. You're getting a little too close to the gate, one of the officers said on the bullhorn, for such a small craft. I'd keep her east a ways. Tide's moving out, and if it takes you out there, you'll capsize.

Thanks, guys! Olivera said. We'll start back.

Paulie fell asleep against his fishing pole and dreamed about May. She leaned over him in the apartment, which was now in San Francisco, and asked him to tell her what time she was in. I am always make the wrong time, she said. The problem, Paulie told her, had to do with their being in two different zones. He woke in the dark and heard his uncle's voice. Lu was squatting beside him, talking about starting life all over again. He was saying something about getting up after you've been dusted by a beanball, getting the courage to swing away at the next pitch because there's always another pitch. You understand what I'm saying?

Paulie grunted yes.

We're not beat. This life's not going to beat us. Your Uncle

Ciso, he's got Lady Luck in his goddamned pocket. The two of us, we got to hustle, but we ain't beat.

That's it, Olivera said. He was pointing his binoculars at a huge ship that had just crossed under the Golden Gate Bridge from the high seas. Goddamn it, that is it.

Ciso drove the boat, with its boxy cathedral hull, straight for the towering ship until Olivera told him to veer right. He veered and honked and flashed a couple of times, and kept going long after Olivera and Lu told him to stop. The ship passed them not more than thirty feet away, like a city block of small windows and massive walls sliding past along the San Andreas Fault, carving the black liquid surface between them. It hid the hills and the city and the moon for a while, and it took their breath away with its size and speed. The men gaped in silence until it passed.

The wake hit them, and their little boat bucked and nearly tipped over. Water slapped and sprayed them. Olivera screamed for Paulie to grab the bucket and bail, and Lu yelled at Ciso to keep it straight as the next wave charged them.

They yelled and floundered, they were soaked and shivering. Son of a bitch, Lu cried. You can't see a damned thing, Jimmy! He swung the little spotlight across the bow. You see anything, Ciso? Did anybody see anything fall off the ship?

They cruised in circles for fifteen minutes, cursing, pointing at anything visible, shivering. Then Ciso said he thought he saw something.

They crept up on the barrel. Olivera raged about how they

were all supposed to be lashed together. He had Paulie reach over the side and grab it with a fisherman's gaff. Should have a little fucking crown painted on the side, he said. Paulie and Lu strained and managed to get it aboard, and as they did Lu saw the delicate painting of a golden crown placed atop tobacco leaves. He hooted with joy.

The other five were close to each other, and Paulie and Lu nearly fell in the drink getting them aboard. Now there was no room for passengers, so the three older men crowded onto Ciso's seat and a barrel, and Paulie lay across the bow, holding on to the cleats in front of the windshield. They headed east, with Alcatraz Island looming before them.

A few minutes later the engine quit. Olivera said it was probably just out of gas, and the spare was next to the motor, but the gas can had disappeared, probably when they'd been swamped. Lu climbed over the barrels and hunted for it. All of the men cursed, and Olivera found a length of rope and secured the barrels to the boat while Lu straddled the motor and checked the carburetor and plugs. They drifted in silence.

Paulie looked at the bridge. Cars and trucks were crossing a thousand feet above the water. They were floating toward the Golden Gate now, toward the ocean, and the boat was rocking more and more as it drifted west. We got paddles? Ciso asked.

Paddles, Olivera said. Son of a bitch.

Lu gave up on the motor and climbed over the barrels. The swells were pitching them up and down.

We're heading for the fucking potato patch, Olivera shouted.

What's the fucking potato patch? Lu asked through clacking teeth.

We get out there, we capsize, like the man said. It's almost to the point of our money or our lives, we gotta signal for help and hope it's some Japanese who don't ask questions.

How do you signal for help? Lu asked.

Ain't you got no flares on this, Ciso? I thought I had a fucking flare gun on this!

This is my first time out, Ciso said. I don't know nothin', Jimmy.

Then we flash the lights and make a lot of racket.

They flashed the little headlight. The boat dipped and lifted over the black waves, and at the crest of each they yelled at distant boat lights. A whirring sound started near Paulic's foot, and he heard Uncle Narciso whoop.

Hey, Ciso said, I got a bite!

Lu wanted to know what the hell he was talking about. In the darkness the men could barely see a mounted reel spinning out. I put a chunk of meat on the hook, he said.

Ciso, you think we give a rat's ass about a fish right now? The boat rocked violently.

I put a hunk of prosciutto on it, Ciso said. The reel whirred and stopped. Ciso tried to crank it. Lu, I got something big, he said.

We're going to drown in the ocean, and you're thinking about a fish?

This is a huge guy, Lu. It won't budge. He strained on the handle. The boat dipped on the side where Ciso's reel was mounted, and the men leaned the other way instinctively. It dipped further and changed directions, and Lu and Jimmy had to climb the barrels, and Paulie had to hang over the other side of the bow, to keep it from flipping over.

Holy Mary Fucking Mother of God, Olivera said. Ciso caught Moby Dick!

Lu peered at his brother, who sat sideways at the helm with one hand on the wheel and the other lighting a damp cigarette with his Zippo. Old Lucky Pants. Sitting there as if this were the most natural thing in the world, to steer an overloaded boat tipped on its side that was being towed by a whale or a goddamned sea monster or a fucking nuclear submarine, in exactly the right direction. They were creeping back toward Alcatraz.

Ciso exhaled a cloud of smoke. I wonder what the hell we got? he said.

The waves became smaller, and the boat moved slowly, towed by some underwater leviathan. Olivera and Lu started laughing hysterically, like children. The son of a bitch is taking us to the Rock, Lu said. Your fish gonna take us home or turn us in to the warden, Ciso?

Hell if I know, Lu. Hell if I know.

Slowly the men and barrels neared Alcatraz Island, which had been recently occupied by American Indians in opposition to the American government. The lighthouse was dark, but the center of the island flickered with dim waves of light. Lu felt a deep pounding in his chest and his head. His heart pounded so hard his head and feet resonated, and it seemed the entire ocean and the sky beat to the same rhythm. And then he heard the voices, faintly at first. Strange, otherworldly voices warbled with his heart's beat. All four men listened as they neared the island. For a moment the drumming and chanting held them transfixed. Then the boat listed a measure lower, and Ludovico's dream of cigars and money was over.

The boat turned itself upside down slowly, like a sleeper turning over on a bed, and they were swallowed by the utter black and cold of the ocean. At first Lu kept a grip on one of the barrels in the black water, but soon he knew the game was up. He didn't know that five of the barrels lashed to the boat and sinking in the bay were filled with cigars and the sixth with a small bale of marijuana packed around a hundred thousand dollars and fifty pounds of cocaine. He didn't know that a month from then Jimmy Olivera would be found floating near the Bay Bridge in a drum like the ones that had held the narcotics and cigars, his head, legs, and arms placed beside his torso in the little tub like parts for assembling.

Lu lost up from down in the dark water, but he didn't struggle. The die was cast, and he would be taken one way or the other, he thought, soon as God or what-the-fuck-ever made up its celestial mind. *What-the-fuck-ever:* this made him laugh and nearly drown. He thought of saying this to the priests of his childhood, and after some time of stasis he felt himself drawn upward, laughing underwater. He rose slowly with aching lungs and gained the surface spluttering, then turned and floated on his back, exhausted, so body-weary he felt unable to ever move his arms again. He heard distant voices come and go. He was aware of his brother and nephew and Olivera swimming to the island, no more than fifty yards away, and he knew he should join them, but he wanted to rest a while first. The ocean held him, his head cupped in its hands. *What-the-fuck-ever, who art in Heaven, hallowed be thy name.* A few wet stars burned in the limitless night above him, and he thought he might be falling into a kind of sleep, and he thought that would be all right.

And maybe death was only a kind of sleep like this. Maybe the hand-painted signs on the loading dock reading *Indian Property* and *Red Power,* the people pounding a flat drum and singing, the heat of the bonfire soaking into his bare arms and legs were also a dream. Jimmy cursing, Paulie shivering in the arms of a young woman who looked exactly like the boy's sister Penelope in some crazy hippie-Indian headband, Narciso dancing a jig by the fire, a sixty-three-year-old *paisano* capering to Indian music in a blanket and argyle socks, spinning around with his arms out like bat wings, displaying his jockey shorts in the flickering light.

Maybe the stairway and the woman, too. The music of the island beat like a drug through his blood vessels, echoed as he groped along a crumbling concrete wall. He followed her across a catwalk in the darkness above the circle of singers and drummers, and near the top of a guard tower she touched his hand, and in the dim light she looked like his wife. When he called her by that name she smiled, and his heart lifted into the heavens like a gull, and her black and ghostly white hair filled with the wind, and her small feet floated above the surface of the earth.

THE TARANTULA

Janine

anine Verbicaro awoke her third morning in Italy, on the train from Rome to Reggio Calabria, sensing the imminence of death. She had the meningitis symptoms, and they were progressing rapidly: splitting headache, neck so stiff she could barely move it, fever chills, a general ache throughout her body. She knew she needed treatment, but what could she do now that she was on the train to the hinterlands? Upright in a crowded compartment, she'd slept with her mouth open and head bent over a rucksack. The Italian family squeezed beside her, skinny little bug-eyed man, plump, scowling wife, and four squirming kids aged about seven to one, had tried to keep a little distance from the sick American girl most of the night, but now it seemed that they had given up. In fact, one of the tots played with her hat, and the man pressed his bony knee into her leg and snapped his Italian newspaper across her pack. He flicked on the small lamp, and Janine's vision of the world outside was perceived through a reflection of her own face on the glass, a narrow face with a prominent nose, small chin, and dark eyes. She stared at her face and the passing hills visible through it, the limestone and twisted oak, and thought of God, and death, and transient beauty, and how much she'd like to place her thumbs beneath the Adam's apple of the little man next to her and squeeze.

Italian men, by genus, by her second day in the old country, ranked somewhere between gopher snakes and poodles. In her first hour among the seven hills and hundred fountains of Roma, her ass had gotten pinched five times. This low estimation didn't encompass the men of her own family, however; nor did it extinguish the romance she had for the country of her progenitors. Mascagni's Cavalleria Rusticana, Albinoni's Adagio for Strings, and another Italian romance she couldn't name played over and over in her mind, the strings and harps in slow waltz time, swaying as the train swayed, winding its way along the rugged coast as her life followed its own winding path to its end.

The youngest grandchild in a large clan of American descendants of Italian immigrants, Janine wanted desperately to love Italy. The grandfather had died when she was a baby, and the grandmother, Rosari Cara Vebicaro, whom she idolized above all others in her family, was nearly a century in age now, in the mid-1980s, in Ronald Reagan's America. What Janine hoped for was an epiphany, an escape from the ugliness of her own culture, some holy moment in the old country, followed by a chance to come home and share her vision of Calabria with her little *nona,* who had been raised there. Now, stroking her pained neck, she thought a phone call to California might be her only chance of expressing this moment of illumination before death intervened.

In her California bungalow, Rosari Verbicaro had a long-legged stove under which slept a scruffy toy poodle named Pepe, the third such in a succession of dogs with the same name. Her oldest daughter, Francesca, leaned over a pot above the dog, and the light through a prune tree in the window moved across the poodle's snout and the daughter's legs and the wall like water in the old woman's memory, like the ocean reflected off the cliffs and grottoes of Calabria. She drifted into reverie while her daughter chattered and stirred. Swaddled by a quilt, the old woman sat in the rocker and remembered a day walking along the beach with her mother in Italy nearly ninety years ago, and she sighed loudly. What is it, Ma? Francesca turned to ask, alarmed.

What?

You all right?

Why wouldn't I be? Keep stirring or it'll spoil.

Francesca laughed. And this was when there interposed upon the reverie and the watery light of a California morning the shape of a huge spider. It moved like a black hand gathering yarn. Holy smokes, the old woman said. Frankie, there's a *tarantella* come to get you.

The daughter, who was also an old lady, screamed and dropped the ladle. Pepe barked and ran around her legs a few times, finally settling on the ladle. The spider crept up the pipe from the stove, up toward the high ceiling. Rosari told her to get the broom and whack it, but Francesca cowered behind her mother before summoning the nerve to approach it. By then the beast was high on the back of the old stovepipe. Watch you don't knock dust into the pot, Rosari told her.

At that moment Janine wrapped a wool scarf around her pained neck and stepped from the coach onto the soil of Calabria. It didn't look at all like the crumpled map she held, or feel like the fantasy she had fostered. The station was dull, drained of color, and it stank of raw sewage. The first impression didn't portend well. Janine was intuitive, random-abstract, and she relied on portents. She was artistically gifted but a little wobbly with directions and helpless with foreign languages. She wasn't very good at math, either, and converting dollars to Italian lira and figuring out how to get to the ancestral village from a station where nobody seemed to understand English was daunting. Nevertheless, and in spite of her father's advice about hiring a driver, she decided to rent a motor scooter for some indecipherable amount of money, from a man with eyes like her Uncle Ludovico's, and drive to the little hill town.

She stuffed her map into the rucksack against a long baguette, her dictionaries, her sketch pad, and her men's shaving bag filled with prescription drugs and naturopathic remedies. She pulled the mannish roadster cap down to her eyebrows and throttled the scooter. A cluster of men gave her advice and directions about operating the Vespa. So far the men of the South weren't the pigs of

Rome, but they all seemed to regard her with an expression some-where between predation and disbelief. Who was this weird, rich American woman in a man's pants and hat? In her midtwenties, and yet she was childless, unmarried? Perhaps they could see the Italian in her face and guess that she was here to see family. Perhaps they could see something in her eyes which revealed how weird she really was.

The city had cobbled streets with chuckholes and piles of pig dung, and she maneuvered among these obstacles without turning her head because of the spinal meningitis. She made blind turns, once nearly crashing into a Volkswagen truck heaped with vegeta-bles, and headed out of town. At the first fork in the highway she took the wrong turn.

An hour later she came around a bend and saw a town built on and into cliff walls. Janine was so startled she killed the motor and got off. Muddy brown brick and mortar were slapped over the precipice, making it difficult in places to distinguish between the work of man and the work of God. Shuttered windows seemed to open out of the earth. Clotheslines stretched across chasms, from stunted pine to rusted balcony. She took out her sketch pad, her loaf of bread, and some cheese she'd bought en route.

Janine had a fine hand and a facile talent with visual arts, and her work attracted the interest of a couple of women trudging up the road who rested from their labor of balancing firewood on their heads to peer over her shoulder. She guessed they were mother and daughter, the latter a beautiful woman in her twenties with a long, delicate nose and bushy eyebrows which accentuated a mischievous look. What did that look mean? She couldn't understand a word they said. She gestured, they spoke, she shook her head and shrugged, they laughed. The young woman leaned over her, the loose sleeveless dress billowing in a warm gust of wind, and Janine inhaled the aroma of the girl's bush of armpit hair. Taking the scarf off her head, the woman shook her black hair out and posed coquettishly. Janine drew her face quickly, as she had done the faces of children and old men in Rome the previous day. She smiled at her own work before handing it over.

She helped carry the firewood to their home in the cliff village, piling much of it across the saddle of the Vespa and standing on the running board. This evoked a lot of stares from the men in the piazza. The older woman and two men of her age took her by the elbows and led her to a dinner table for a feast which lasted almost three hours. It appeared that a dozen neighbors or relatives followed and joined in as they ate, including an old matriarch who took the seat of honor at one end, and all the while the family of eight or a dozen laughed and spoke while Janine and the young woman, whose name was Marie, exchanged furtive glances across the table.

The mother held up the drawing of her daughter, and the audience oohed and ahed. Although Janine understood almost none of the language, the expressions and gestures of the people at table were so familiar that she felt she'd already heard this entire conversation and understood it perfectly, sitting among her aunts and uncles in her grandmother's house many nights near the San Francisco Bay.

In California, the spider walked across the kitchen wall again the next day when another daughter, Grazia, was having coffee and feeding the old woman porridge. Rosari's second daughter threw a pepper mill at it. Pepe ran from the room and knocked the screen door open, and the tarantula scuttled quickly following the racket. Grazia charged and barely missed ending its life with a frying pan.

Rosari watched the spectacle and realized that it wasn't after Francesca, or Grazia, or even Pepe. It thinks I'm ready to kick the bucket, she told her daughter.

You're not kicking any bucket, Ma.

Oh, yes, I am, Little Sally Sunshine. The *tarantella* knows it, too.

He's the one who's kicking the bucket, Ma. Next time he sticks his nose out I'll squish him like a grape.

The little old woman stared at the wall. Her white hair was so thin it floated above her scalp like a baby's. She touched her daughter's hand. You know what your father did? He brought home these bananas which he would eat like a monkey, she said.

Papa?

He climbed like one, too. You ever seen him pruning the trees? A gorilla with his bananas.

Not my papa, the daughter admonished, trying not to laugh.

That's the way he did things. He tears down a house with the big hammer, and you see him swing up there like Tarzan of the Apes and shout he wants his lunch.

Grazia laughed and shook her head. She was the smallest and most jovial of the daughters, a lively swing dancer, even in her late sixties, mother of four children, grandmother of seven. So, he yells for lunch?

Yes. I threw him a banana. What's your son up to?

Which one?

I forget the names.

They're fine, Ma. They're busy, all three of them.

So, he finds one right there one day, and he jumps so high you think he's a bullfrog.

I don't understand. Grazia tried to feed Rosari more porridge. He finds what, Ma?

One of them, come on the banana boat. Oh, you don't think that one knows?

Knows what, Ma?

It's my time.

Don't say that, Mama. It's his time, not yours.

Hey, what do you think I am, Methuselah? He knows.

Janine slept in the family's cellar, and when she woke it seemed that her spinal meningitis had evolved to Hodgkin's disease. Her neck was no longer so stiff, but its glands were swollen, and she was sweating and feverish, and her skin felt itchy. She had other symptoms as well: weakness, fatigue, weight loss. She consulted the dog-eared medical dictionary and wondered if she'd need to go back to Rome for the radiation therapy. It was all a matter of time and luck.

The mother and daughter could see that she wasn't well, and they made her drink something bitter and lie under a pile of blankets. They showed her photographs of the young woman, and from these she started to piece together a story: Marie was the widow of the man in the wedding picture featured on their mantel under black bunting, and Lucia, the toddler who usually balanced on her hip and squished pasta in her fist at the table, was her daughter, not her sister. Straight, knocked up, married, widowed. Damn, thought Janine, what a waste. She herself had only dated a few guys and then, in college, a few girls, far from home and the eyes of an enormous extended Italian American family in the Bay Area. Her sexual orientation was a Rosetta stone hidden in some cave, unknown to the parents and aunts and cousins who kept setting her up with eligible bachelors, though she hoped, she imagined, that her little grandmother somehow understood.

Marie leaned over Janine and sponged her brow, and the sad beauty of that face, the look of so many Italian women who hold their young and their dying loved ones like Mary holding Jesus in the *pieta,* stung her to the quick. Then that mischievous sidelong glance, that hidden joke, and the little pinch to her cheek: What was the woman thinking? Janine's heart fluttered in its cage.

The symptoms changed to severe abdominal cramps and diarrhea that afternoon. It was now reasonable to assume that she had Crohn's disease instead of Hodgkin's, given the evidence. This was a relief of sorts. However, further reading informed her that cholera was a possibility, too, especially in this part of the world.

Two days of being nursed and staring up into Marie's face

passed, and Janine got off the bed and the toilet and didn't die. She felt well enough to find a telephone, and gestured to her ear, and Marie led her to the scooter (which one of the brothers had been using quite a bit) and got on the back. The family didn't have a phone, but there was a telephone office next to the post. Janine spoke with her mother about Rosari and learned that her father's family was in a heated debate about letting her die at home or putting her in a hospital. What about Marge, the nurse who came by? Janine wanted to know. Well, half the family says Marge has it made in the shade, her mother said. The sisters do all the work, and she comes by to take her pulse and gets paid a bundle. How about you? Are you sick?

I'm all right.

You sound sick. How do you know if you're all right?

I'm tired, Mama.

That usually means you're sick. Are you eating oranges?

Of course.

Janine and Marie took Lucia on the scooter to the market and bought oranges, then rode into the mountains and walked across a cornfield. They sat together and played with the little one and shared an orange and pointed at things with the segments, a distant stone hut, the face of a mountain. They said the names for things, repeating each other's words. Marie opened her dress and nursed Lucia until the little one fell asleep. Janine watched breathlessly.

They looked through the sketch book and spoke of America. Now and then the young woman's hand fell on hers, or her milky breast pressed against her shoulder. Janine put her arm around her waist, and Marie kissed her cheek. Friends, they said to each other. They kissed, mouth to mouth. The bushy eyebrows rose. Lonely, they said to each other. They kissed again and laughed.

Marie's hair came unfastened and mingled with the grass and corn litter. They snuggled together, wrapped in each other's arms, with the baby between. Friends. Marie's eyes closed, and she opened her dress again to let the sun strike her breasts. Janine trembled to see her beauty. They sunned together in the swaying light of corn leaves and nearly fell asleep embracing in the warm breeze until the spider intruded.

Marie sat up with a sudden shriek that awoke Lucia. The hairy arachnid dropped from her hair, and Janine crushed it into a paste with the top of her roadster cap. Marie grabbed her neck and wept onto her bare knees. They buttoned up quickly and returned to her home.

The old woman's days and nights were becoming much the same, propped in a recliner or rocker under quilts or sitting up in bed, talking to family or looking for the dark shape to appear above the stove. Her sons and sons-in-law took a crack at it and discussed poison gas and traps. Her eldest, Narciso, brought his grandson's dart gun and hit Pepe with one on a practice shot. She shook her head and lost track of their names and faces. She shrugged dramatically. What can you do? There are some things where there is nothing you can do.

It waited for them to leave and came to her bedroom some nights, a black hand creeping across the ceiling. She told it to shoo. Go back to your bananas, she said. Sometimes she couldn't tell if it were there or not. Shadows moved the same way near the Venetian blinds and the bed lamp, from the window with the Japanese maple. I'm not scared of you, she said in Italian. Her youngest daughter sat on the bed beside her and asked what was wrong. When Mary looked and couldn't see it, Rosari realized that sometimes only she could. Hey! *Baciagalupe,* she said. *Kiss of the wolf!* Get out of here.

Sometimes her children gathered in the living room to discuss her death when they thought she was asleep, the eldest ones silver-haired old men and women themselves, shuffling on unsteady knees or coughing up decades of cigarette smoke. They raised their voices to make a point, laughed, cooed like mourning doves. Hey, Ludovico, she yelled, and her second son hurried to her side.

Ma's awake, he said. Hey, how's my mama doing? You look like a million bucks, Ma!

Right. And you're the king of Prussia. Listen, did what's-her-name feed Pepe that calamari?

Calamari? You feeding squid to that dog, Ma?

Who's here? Who's in the house? I heard you because you got the loudest mouth.

We're all here, Ma. The whole family's here.

How about the old man. I thought I heard him, too.

Ludovico's voice broke. Papa? Ma, Papa's been gone for twenty-five years.

Oh, yeah? She stared at her little hands. I thought I heard him in there.

Back in her home Marie wept and pulled her hair back to show her mother her neck. Her brothers ran off, and Janine assumed it was to fetch a doctor. Meanwhile, the mother held the toddler and spread several rags and scarves across a bed, and Marie fingered them like tomatoes in the market. She would lift one near her nose, then put it down. More scarves and garments were placed on the bed, including Janine's black wool neck-warmer, each with its own hue. Janine took off her cap, and the young woman seized it and turned it inside out to expose the bright red lining. This she clutched to her bosom.

Two scrawny old men came with the brothers. They carried musical instruments instead of doctors' bags. Janine was puzzled by the rapid verbal exchanges, the rearrangement of the furniture to clear a space around the girl. Marie swayed back and forth, and the bald old men began playing various squeaky tunes on a violin with tambourine accompaniment, each piece a mournful jig, to which the young woman moved her hips and arms. It seemed that one melody was finally the right one for her because she leaped and capered around the room to it. The fiddler played this same tune over and over, and the girl closed her eyes and danced madly.

A third man arrived with an old guitar with only five strings.

He cried out and shrugged, and it seemed that the guitar was handed to everybody in the room except the girl until it landed in Janine's lap. Self-taught on guitar, she tuned it and immediately mimicked the violinist, to the obvious glee of the assemblage. She plucked the jumpy melody note for note and put chords to it. The two men and Janine kept playing without variation for the rest of that day, and Marie danced and moaned in the center of the room.

Lanterns were lit, and the music and dance continued. Janine's arms ached and her brow dripped sweat onto the strings, but she kept playing, as did the old violinist and tambourine player. These men had sunken eyes and push-broom mustaches, and their perfor-mance was mechanical and somber, even if the tune was lively. Now and then Janine found a way to make the smallest embellishment on the melody, the slightest brush stroke of variation. The girl's sweat mingled with the smells of candles and lantern oil. She shivered and spun, shook her hips and arms, and rubbed her face with Janine's inside-out cap. A couple of times she opened her dress enough to nurse Lucia while rocking her hips slowly in dance.

Janine's fingers ached and her fever raged and abated, but she kept playing, and the girl kept dancing, and the old men kept work-ing at their instruments like coal miners under the whip. She watched Marie's face turn gaunt, bloodless, waxen. Sometimes the room appeared to spin around her stationary body. Sometimes her hands flew about the room independent of her arms and left streams of colors in the air.

When Janine closed her eyes she was in a dark church. It was not the church of her childhood in California, but similar, a cool and musty place of darkness and incense. Instead of the crucified savior there was a dying woman on the cross whose face kept changing, and Janine felt herself fly about the rafters, up to this sorrowful figure, but she could never quite get the face right. She might be Marie; she might be Janine's oldest sister, the one who'd disappeared long ago; she might be her grandmother as a young woman. Then again, she might be a woman who'd lived in these mountains and had been killed by the men who feared or hated her for being strange to them.

A new day's first light wove its beams through the window blinds, and the lanterns were snuffed. All night they had made the *tarantella* until, at first light, the young woman suddenly stopped and opened her eyes, as if awakening from a dream, and told the musicians to go home. So haggard was she that Janine imagined Marie an old woman for a moment. The guitar was placed on the floor, gently, a warm thing vibrating life, as the two young women collapsed beside it.

everal thousand miles away the little grandmother listened to the voices of family and watched the black fingers move above her until she smiled. The shadowy movement was not the *baciagalupe*, the painful kiss-of-the-wolf love of her ne'er-do-well husband, Giuseppe, entreating her to come once again to his side. It's *you,* she said.

Her granddaughter set the instrument down and lay on the cold floor and held the hand of a strange young woman in a strange land. She surrendered to the ageless sorrow and mystery of those who elect to share their hearts, against danger and prejudice, while the grandmother watched the spider's legs take the shape of a woman's tresses floating in a bath, floating behind the head of a woman who'd died more than eighty years ago. She smiled and opened her heart. *Ciao, Mama,* she said.

THE ISLAND OF PELICANS

Samantha

ngelo's wife left him for their chiropractor that spring, and though they hadn't begun mediation he had unofficial custody of their eight-year-old daughter, Samantha, for the month of June. He took her to visit his family in the Bay Area and talked up the excitement of the chocolate factory, the cable cars, and some place his daughter remembered where you could Whack a Mole with what she thought was a tortilla-shaped hammer. Pier 39 was a showcase for linguistic cute, and it made Angelo's flesh crawl reading the signs. *I Left My Harp in San Francisco. It's My Parsley, and I'll Cry if I Want To. Between a Rock and a Hard Roll Pretzels.*

Why is that an *especially* cute name, Daddy? They were at the end of the pier, giving money to the cart vendor.

Well, you can see Alcatraz Island right there, he said, as well as on this cute pretzel logo. Alcatraz was called the Rock, and it meant a lot of different things to prisoners and to the Indians who tried to take it back in 1970, and because everybody agrees that it was such a cute prison nobody thinks much about the quality of the pretzel or whether or not it's hard as a rock, they just buy it and laugh.

Samantha stared across the bay at the island and the sailboats. You're being sarcastic again, she said.

No, not me. Never.

He had to carry her on his shoulders part of the way to Ghirardelli Square because the tourists loitered in huge clumps. Occasionally a woman with his wife's hair or figure would pass, and his heart would palpitate. The sensation was less like grief or longing than panic, as if some nemesis had tracked him down and were poised for attack. He made a rude comment about some people paying to take a picture with a cross-dresser, and Samantha giggled. This used to be a neighborhood, he told his daughter, where people actually lived. Your great-grandparents, your grandpa and all of his brothers and sisters, they actually lived here and bought groceries on the wharf. We used to hang out here, before the entire city became a theme park.

This isn't a theme park, she said.

Oh, it is, the city council voted to make it a theme park. You park and pay to get in, and all the people who aren't tourists are actors. You saw the guy in the pink dress and mustache.

Right. Where are the rides, then?

Tour boats to see the cute prison. Genuine turn-of-the-century cable cars, genuine Chinese and Italian people talking funny.

Turn of what century?

That means the end of the Gay '90s and beginning of the 1900s.

The Gay Pride started in the '90s?

Angelo chuckled breathlessly. You could probably say that and get away with it, he said. His shoulders ached, and he wondered for the five hundredth time if becoming a father at age forty-five had been such a good idea. With his wife, soon-to-be-ex-wife, Jennifer, it had seemed like the *only* idea. They'd taken infant brain development and midlife memory-loss workshops, slipped on bifocals before pinning diapers.

Angelo followed a crowd of people holding camcorders through an obstacle course of stationary homeless vagrants, even stepping over one man on a grate. The rich smells of roasted garlic and coffee filled his nostrils. Okay, he panted, as I believe you know, your great-grandparents came here from Italy and lived in this neighborhood about a hundred years ago. *That* was the turn of the century.

Why isn't *this* the turn of the century?

From Angelo's knapsack came a muffled tinkling. Angelo found a vacant square of brick on the edge of a fountain, and Samantha pulled the small laptop out. Hey, it's Aunt Naomi! Tell her we're at the chocolate factory!

Don't call her your aunt, Angelo said. She's my Jewish fairy godmother.

Why is she your Jewish fairy godmother?

She's just kind of out there flapping her wings.

I thought you liked her.

I do like her, but sometimes she pisses me off. I don't know, some people in big cities do things that cause a wake of pain in other people's lives and waltz away like it's nothing. Maybe it's just New Yorkers in general.

Whatever. Did she sell your Wyoming screenplay to Hollywood?

Let me read this. Huh.

Naomi asked about his family, as she always did, before she got down to business, which was really not much to report. A producer on location in Wyoming was excited but not committed. He already knew that.

Hey, Monkey, Angelo said as he put the laptop away, do me a favor. When you get married, don't hyphenate your name to something horrible like Naomi Ginsburg-Menendez. It sounds like a yuppie bar where they serve matzo burritos.

I'm not getting married!

Well, not this week. How badly do you want a hot-fudge sundae?

Badly. You never answered my question. Samantha climbed onto his shoulders. The line stretched from the chocolate factory restaurant's doors to the edge of the fountain in the bricked square. She took her shoes off and waded among the turtle sculptures. Why isn't *this* the turn of the century?

I guess you could call it that and get away with it.

Who is that man? He keeps staring at me.

Don't look at him. What man? What's he look like? Angelo bent over the edge of the fountain and held his daughter's shoulders, peering across the water and turtles at the crowd of people.

I can't tell you if I don't look at him.

Okay, look quickly, then look away.

Samantha's eyes darted to the side, then returned to her father's face. Didn't see him. Oh, wait. He's right behind you.

Angelo turned. The sun was in his eyes, but he made out the figure of a tall, broad-shouldered man with a long white beard, so bushy that it glowed like a halo. A vagrant. Yes? Angelo said.

She's beautiful, the man said.

Excuse me? Angelo said.

She looks like Penny. Her eyes, I mean. The mouth is like Nona Rosari's.

Angelo stood. Paulie, for Christ's sake! He hugged the man and felt himself simultaneously lifted off his feet and overwhelmed by his odor. Samantha, he croaked, this is your uncle, my older brother, Paulie.

It's Paul now. He reached to shake her hand across a yard of water.

What do you mean, I can't call you Paulie? You're not a kid anymore?

No. I got the word that, from now on, I am Paul.

Who said it? Samantha wanted to know.

The Lord told me. Clear as I'm talking to you right now.

Great, Angelo said, clapping his hands, the line is finally moving. He grabbed Samantha's shoes, and she climbed onto his neck above the knapsack. Her little hands were wet on his balding scalp.

You think God talks to you? she asked.

Yes. He stood an arm's length from them, next to the line, and stared at Samantha. Angelo noticed the way the young couple in front of them, an attractive pair in matching spandex bicycle outfits, glanced at each other and chuckled. Now and then He does, Paul said.

Are you my uncle who came back crazy from a war? The spandex couple covered their mouths.

Honey, he wasn't crazy, what your mama and I said is he was addicted to a drug when he came back, which makes people feel crazy, but he got well. I'm sorry, Paulie

Paul. No, it's okay, because she's right. I was crazy after 'Nam. I was obsessed with death and getting high. I was a junkie until Jesus healed me on the island, and that's when I started doing the Lord's work.

The line surged forward several yards, and Angelo didn't know, as they neared the door, whether he should encourage more conversation in this vein or beg off. Excuse me for asking, he said after an awkward lull, but which Jesus are we talking about, Paulster? Jesús, or *Jesus?*

I'd like to talk with you about that.

Daddy always yells Jesus when he's mad, Samantha said. Or Jesus Christ on a pogo stick.

Paul stared soberly at the girl a moment, too long a moment for normal, then bellowed laughter. Your father is the funniest person I know. What does he do for a living? Does he write jokes?

He writes ads. We bought our house, Mom's and my house now, on a deodorant ad.

Never mind that, Angelo said. Sweat crept across his brow. Spandex guy's eyes rolled back, and Angelo asked him if he'd ever considered using a deodorant himself, and the guy turned away. Samantha told her uncle, in a very loud voice, that her father had written these ten words and gotten paid a pile of money: *Because it's never too late to make a first impression.*

Paul stroked his white beard and gazed above Samantha's head. Angelo thought he looked like an Italian John Muir, or an old Civil

War vet photographed at the fifty-year reunion at Gettysburg, some geezer who would hold a megaphone to his ear. Finally he said that it didn't make any sense to him at all.

It's not supposed to make sense, exactly. The spandex people squeezed inside. It's supposed to sell deodorant, and they paid me enough to put a down payment on a house. Listen, you want to join us?

Samantha climbed down from her father's shoulders and touched her uncle's huge belt buckle, a battered plate of brass with horses on it. Did you know, she said, that this is the turn of the century?

Paul stared at his little brother. No, he said. I didn't know that.

The two men began the story of the Jesús they knew for Samantha's benefit, the Jesús with their last name, not the famous guy who'd died on the cross and started Christmas decorations and Easter-egg hunting, Angelo said. He told his daughter that her great-grandfather had left her great-grandmother for a young Mexican woman, who'd given birth to Jesús, here in North Beach. After the old man died, this Jesús and his mother took off for migratory farm work and disappeared until he was about eighteen and wandering around San Francisco, kind of like your Uncle Paulie seems to be doing now, when he ran into our sister and got reconnected with the family.

Paul.

Paul. That was what, thirty-three, thirty-five years ago? So, he becomes kind of an Indian cult leader, and our aunt gets him a job cleaning the church with me.

You cleaned up a church?

Part-time, while I was going to college and doing guerrilla theater with a bunch of wacky friends.

You did gorilla theater, dressed up as gorillas?

You could say that and get away with it, yes. Political monkey
theater, mostly about Dick Nixon and Spiro Agnew. Anyway, Jesús:
technically, he was our uncle, or step-uncle, even though he was
younger than either Paulie or myself.

Paul.

Right. You know, you're lucky God didn't name you Ali Bag-
man or something, like this friend of Sam's mom. This way you
don't have to change your ID or anything.

Was the church dirty?

The church was filthy, you wouldn't believe what slobs those
Catholics were. Gum stuck to the bottom of the pews, mud on the
kneeling pads. Hey, Paulie, Paul, you okay?

His brother was standing now in the middle of the crowded
restaurant, his eyes closed. He didn't answer at first, and Angelo
and Sam exchanged looks. Then he said he needed to get going, but
he'd come by their mother's house later tonight. Yes, tonight. Angelo stood to hug him again, but Paul was off, his head down and
cocked to one side as if he were listening for something.

Okay, Angelo yelled. Tonight. I'll tell Ma.

Their mother's house in the East Bay depressed him, and he rarely
stayed there for long. A palpable decrepitude was what Jennifer
had said of the place, and he wondered now if the way his mom

lived had contributed to Jenn's decision to leave him. It was a shrine to loss, a place to remember lost children and lost marriage, and symbols of these losses lay about under dust and cobwebs. High school portraits of Angie's brother Paulie and sister Penny, the two that had been missing or drifting aimlessly for over thirty years now; a chipped dining room set and yellowed curtains from the World War II years when his folks had married; his late sister Mickey's bedroom, left intact, arrested in a childhood of Down syndrome that had lasted nearly thirty years. Only he and his little sister had escaped complete ruin and left recent photos of grandchildren and new cars from their homes five hundred miles north and south of here. While the photos of Angelo and his sister Janine (whose homosexuality remained secret to their parents) turned gray-templed and bruised-eyed making babies and mortgage payments, the others remained forever young on the mantel.

I haven't seen Paulie in a year, his mother said. She sighed heavily over her wineglass. I won't hold my breath. I'm so glad you boys got to see each other, at least.

Sam called her mom, then gave the phone to Angelo. Jennifer sounded upset, and for a nanosecond of conscious thought Angelo allowed that her sadness was regret, for leaving him, for not being there with her husband and daughter on vacation. No, it had to do with dairy products. Didn't he remember how dairy-sensitive Sam was? Had he forgotten the respiratory infections, the nights they'd stayed up holding her over a vaporizer? He hadn't forgotten. In fact, the memory of sitting up in bed with little Sam and Jennifer made his eyes water. Are you going to make sure she eats something green tomorrow?

I think her grandmother just gave her some green gummy worms.

Angelo, be serious for a change.

Sam slept in Penny's old bed, and Angelo made like a doctor with a thick German accent and listened to her breathing. Du must stop eatink der cow's milch, kinder!

How do you *eat* milk, dummy?

I don't know, but it is verboten!

Dad, please? Seeing the old uncle had made her ever more curious about the mysterious aunt from whom her middle name came, that beautiful young woman above the fireplace who was the family fugitive. Angelo told her a few things about his sister as he rubbed his daughter's back and listened to her breathing. Penny was the smartest one in the family. That might not be saying much, however.

Can the sarcasm, please, Dad. What's a fugitive?

It means you're on the run from the law. Anyway, the reason she's a fugitive is because her crime was taken very seriously by the government.

What does the government care? Sam yawned. It wasn't like she killed somebody, right?

Right. Well, somebody did die by accident when she and some people burned a bunch of property. Anyway, the government cares a lot about certain things, especially during a war.

That's dumb, Sam said before falling asleep.

A few hours later, while Angelo was watching *Letterman,* the doorbell rang. His brother stood on the porch, eyes huge behind glasses held together by electrical tape. The old place, he said.

Angelo offered him a beer, but Paul said he was clean and turned it down. They sat and watched TV for a half hour before Paul spoke again. You ever wonder if Jesus really is God, and if he's still alive?

Which Jesus are we talking about this time?

The one with our last name. Angie, I think I'm close to finding him.

Oh, Christ, Angelo sighed. You mean, you don't think Jesús died? You think it's possible he came back to life?

Came back to life. Why would you think that?

Paul paced in front of the set. Angelo felt a little bit afraid of him, and he thought of things to hit his brother over the head with, should he go ballistic. The padded footstool. The remote. Paulie, Paul, did he really cure your addiction that night on the island? Wait. Let me get another beer, and then you tell me about it, okay?

The Jesús that Paul remembered was a natural leader among the Indians who occupied Alcatraz Island. He wasn't a fiery speaker exactly, but when he spoke about pain and oppression it made your skin crawl, it made the ground underneath you fall away, and you felt this timelessness and selflessness that were a lot like the heroin Paul had been addicted to. And he was physically beautiful, and his touch had an electrical charge and heat on your scalp. That was how the healing started, during the circle drum when Paul was already in a kind of trance from the singing and the rhythm, there on the island at midnight. Their sister Penny was there, like some disciple, and Jesús came up to Paul and placed his hands on his head, and a place in his forehead opened up and let the demon of addiction out and let the source of God's healing in.

He opened your third eye, so to speak. Angelo muted the TV. The screen filled with the face of a young man with hair like meringue.

I don't believe in that third eye stuff, Paul said.

Or, whatever, he let out the bad and let in the good, or something.

Drugs are demonic energy sent to us by Satan. Paul paced again. Our country, this whole fucking world, we are so filled with Satan's seductive drugs!

That oversized book of pictures of classic cars, which the boys had gotten their father as a joint Christmas gift over forty years ago, its cover so sun-bleached now that the Stutz Bearcat was reduced to the ghost of a rolled fender and a few spokes, might stun his brother if he smacked him over the head with it.

Their mother walked in. She gave Paul a hug and castigated him for never coming to see her. What, is it so hard to come across the bay and see your old mother?

I don't live in the city, Ma, I'm just visiting.

Where do you live now?

On that same hippie farm in the Southwest. Sunshine Farm.

Sunshine Farm. Jesus. You were a baby when you left, and you never really came back, Paulie, and I still blame myself for signing that paper.

Pop signed it.

You were underage! You were underage, and they let you go to Vietnam, those bastards. They ruined your life, and Penny's life!

My life's not ruined, Ma.

Yeah, right.

Sure you won't have a beer? Angelo asked. Some leftover gnocchi? His mother and brother stood staring at each other. Oh, Christ. He wanted to grab his daughter and drive back to LA. He wanted to find his brother a job and a therapist, his mother a husband or a roommate or a support group. He walked to the kitchen and opened the fridge, and a teardrop fell on his lens. He wanted his mom to love him as much as she loved Paulie and Penny, her first and most precious babies, her lost lambs.

The next day they went to the city in Angelo's station wagon, a functional-looking Italian American family, he thought, with the guys in front and the gals in back. A cousin's granddaughter, a year older than Samantha, sat between Angelo's daughter and mother and giggled most of the way. He dropped them off at Union Square, in front of Macy's.

Ma, please don't let her put on so much makeup and perfume that some social worker busts my chops, okay?

His mother laughed. She looked happy, perky in her dashiki. She told her boys to enjoy the ballgame, or wherever they were going. Angelo drove through the heavy traffic to the Mission District and found a parking place in a neighborhood of loud colors and Spanish advertisements. He fed four dollars into the meter. So, where's this burrito joint? he asked his brother.

Paul walked in silence, his brow knitted. Angelo had to work to keep up with him. They were walking through what Angelo might call a ghetto, and the boys he saw crowded around a car he would call gang-bangers. Thumping hip-hop blended with salsa, corny organs and melodramatic chords on synthesizers, the word *amor* in a sleazy echo repeated every few seconds, *love, oh, careless love,* he thought, mixed with rap cadences punctuated by *butt, bitch,* and *fuck.* His old soldier/junkie brother, the baseball star, Mr. Strong and Silent, whose exploits on the field had been their father's favorite subject when they'd been kids, marched fearlessly through the valley of gangstas to a taqueria.

All of the other patrons were Mexicans, apparently. Angelo bought them little tacos with radish and lime garnish. He drank a Corona while Paul stuck with water. Paul wanted to stay when they were done eating, so Angelo ordered another beer. A tall man with long white hair entered the restaurant, and Paul went up to hug him.

Jim Littlebear, Paul said, this is my brother, Angelo. He knew Jesús.

Not in the biblical sense, Angelo said. He chuckled and shook the man's hand. Well. Can I buy you a beer? Some tacos?

Jim Littlebear accepted a beer. He and Paul sat and stared at each other for some time, Mona Lisa smiles playing across their lips. Angelo tried to engage them in conversation. You guys should try these fish tacos. Where do you guys know each other from? You live here, Jim? You guys in the same outfit or something?

Their silence became embarrassing to Angelo. He gazed out the window. He pulled out his laptop and checked his mail. He got within one digit of writing his wife. Jim Littlebear walked slowly to the jukebox, which had just finished a Mexican *corrido,* and dropped quarters into it. He smiled as the music started up again: Nights in White Satin. The Moody Blues made no sense to Angelo in a little Mexican taqueria. His brother and Jim Littlebear resumed their postures at the table, now and then closing their eyes and rocking their heads to the music. Both men were silent through the entire song. Angelo found the crapper, which seemed to him imported specially from Tijuana. He could hear the cheerful beat of another ballad from Northern Mexico, then Nights in White Satin again. Gag me with a patchouli stick, Angelo thought. When he came out there were three more people at the table, two of whom were Indian or Mexican women, the third a little white troll with a longer beard than Paul's.

My brother, Angelo, Paul said. Lorna Dee Hernández, Kathy Manslayer, and Roger the Lodger. I don't know your last name, Lodger.

That's cool, nobody does, the little man croaked.

Man slayer? Angelo asked.

My brother knew Jesús, maybe better than I did because they worked together.

The ladies nodded their heads and made oohing sounds. Lorna

Dee was a dark, plump woman with short black hair and thick glasses. Manslayer had long silver-and-black hair which fell across her sharp cheeks. Something in the arc of her neck made him think of Jennifer. Roger asked if anybody besides him was hungry, and Lorna Dee called out to the waitress in Spanish.

I guess we should start, Jim Littlebear said.

Paul said that he guessed they were all as anxious as he was to see Jesús again. Angelo noticed that the younger woman, Lorna Dee, had a puzzled expression on her face as his brother spoke. Paul related the hands-on healing experience, how he'd been cured of heroin addiction.

Amen, Angelo said. He raised his hands in the air. He kept a straight face. A slow Mexican polka with quivering, nasal voices groaned in the background. Plates of beans, tortillas, and rice came to their table. The Lodger dug in.

Lorna Dee's brow remained knitted during Paul's talk and continued its scowl through Littlebear's description of Jesús preaching on Alcatraz. How Jesús had seemed aware of the troubled spirits of the former inmates, how he'd told riddles which you had to puzzle over until they hit you right here, and he struck himself on the head by way of punctuation.

Hallelujah, Angelo said, raising his arms again, trying to catch Lorna Dee's attention. Nobody seemed to notice.

Lorna Dee raised her hand, like a kid in class, and Jim called on her like a teacher. Her maroon nails extended a couple of inches past the tips of her fingers. When Kathy called me, I thought we were going to talk about the newspaper articles, she said.

Newspaper of Jesus, Angelo said, arms rising again.

Kathy Manslayer touched his arm. They were all glaring at him now. Why are you here? When Kathy asked him this, Angelo blushed. It wasn't just her neck, it was the shape of her eyebrows, especially now that she was mad, which made him think of Jennifer. He apologized, but Kathy kept glaring at him.

Okay, he said, I am really sorry. I'll try to be a better person.

I wonder if you really knew him, Kathy said.

Well, I did. We used to make each other laugh when we were supposed to be cleaning the Venetian blinds in the church rectory. You guys talk about him like he was God's only begotten son, but I saw a very human side to him. He could imitate voices, for one thing. He did that Indian shtick as a gag in our guerrilla theater. Paulie, don't you remember he was Mexican and Italian? He just looked like an Indian.

The group at table sat silently for a moment. Even the music stopped, the whining waltzes and polkas about love. Kathy Manslayer stared at Angelo. Finally she asked him why he was such a pessimist.

I'm a pessimist because I don't think our step-uncle, or whatever you want to call him, was the actual son of God?

Negative, Jim Littlebear said. Heads nodded sympathetically.

Angelo felt his face burning. Did you know that I wrote a lot of those riddles Jim was talking about? Jesús and I came up with these enigmatic, pithy sayings together, when we were stoned and doing people's voices. He would do this evangelist act right at the pulpit in our church when we were the only ones there. I used to pretend to be crippled, and he'd say something nonsensical, some puzzler we made up together: *If the pelican catches a fish but cannot swallow it because the fisherman has tied twine about its throat, how does the armadillo dream in his shell?* Then he'd lay his hands on me, and I'd walk away, healed. Sometimes I'd jump and click my heels. Paulie, I'm sorry. He was an actor.

Paul.

Paul! He goofed on people with me, for money! It was an act!

Now, hold on a second. It was the little white troll, Roger the Lodger, who spoke in his sandpaper voice through a mouthful of beans. Hold on. I got by most of my life as a thief and a con man, and I've seen them all. The religious cons, too. This boy might have pulled some con, but what he done, when I seen him, was the real McCoy. I mean . . . Roger spread his arms out and looked up. I mean, you felt it, the energy, man, you felt it!

Jim and Kathy smiled and nodded. He was maybe a little bit the trickster, Jim said, and Kathy laughed. Yes. I think he had the trickster in him, too.

Tricked our sister into setting fire to the draft-board office, Angelo said to himself while the others grinned and nodded. His laptop tinkled, and he walked outside to a sidewalk table to read the message.

Naomi wanted to warn him about the rejection before his copy came in the mail. She always warned him first. He wrote back, thanking her heartily for giving him the bad news. He described the situation in the restaurant and how he needed an excuse to leave the table.

He didn't want to return to the group inside, so he pretended to press the keys. He could see them sitting around the food with their hands joined, now. Manslayer was a beautiful woman, he realized, and in his inimitable way he'd made sure she hated his guts, hadn't he? Now she was holding something, and it looked as though she were reading aloud to the group from a newspaper clipping. The Lodger looked at him, and Angelo pretended to read the screen until the familiar tinkling indicated that he had another message from across the continent.

Naomi asked him how he felt about his brother's desire to find this person. Didn't Angelo want to find Jesús Verbizcaro, too? The story he'd written, and which she'd helped him publish so many years ago in a journal and cited when she offered further representation, was ostensibly about that same young man on Alcatraz Island. Shouldn't he join his brother's search?

Jesús had called Alcatraz La Isla de Alcatraces, which Angelo had translated to The Island of Pelicans as the title of his old story. So, Naomi thought he should join his crazy brother and write a follow-up story on the adventure or something.

Everybody around him was going insane.

He wrote back, asking if Naomi could find an electronic address for the real Jesus in Heaven so Angelo could tell Him about the group of old hippies in the restaurant, and how He might need to appear and set them straight. Poor bastards, they're waiting for you, Big Guy, and they've got you mixed up with my great uncle. Why don't you show, you old trickster? Help my brother, for Christ's sake.

THE ISLAND OF WOMEN

❋

Angelo

❋

hree weeks after the taqueria supper, Angelo stood near the Basilica of the Virgin of Guadalupe in Mexico City and lost his brother. Anvil-shaped clouds gathered above the city as he hurried down the steps they'd just ascended. After an hour of searching he stretched out on a stone ledge, under the once-buried nostrils of a plumed serpent covered by Catholics when they built their church on top of the Indian temple, and moaned. The rain came and drenched him before he could seek shelter.

An old woman leaned over him and asked if he was drunk, *boracho,* he understood that much, and he shook his head.

No puedo encontrar mi hermano, he said.

Su hermano, the woman said, pointing. Angelo looked and saw Paul wandering across the street.

He rushed across a street which flowed now like a stream, and it made him remember something about the original Aztec city being an island with canals. Paul's white hair towered over the mass of people in the open-air market, but Angelo's cries went unheard.

Muddy buses roared by like resurrected dinosaurs, kids kicked balls against crumbling walls, the streets were filled with people, three kids riding one bicycle, mothers and fathers carrying five little ones and three plastic sacks of food between them. Angelo saw a pharmacy with an electric pony in front of it and a line of kids waiting for a ride, like this was the Matterhorn at Disneyland. Above his brother's head he saw a school of fish-shaped *huaraches* nosing up strings to the rafters of the market. He saw human-sized bleeding carcasses on tables, plucked chickens hanging among bananas and shell necklaces; he saw angel-faced children selling corn tortillas from baskets, and toothless beggars, one a leper, he supposed, with a cave for a nose. Paul stood before a stall filled with jars and bundled herbs.

Hey, Angie, where you been?

They boarded the Red Arrow, La Flecha Roja, for Cuernavaca. Mexico City was like two or three Los Angeleses, Angelo thought, a pasta bowl heaped over the rim with smog and people, but what would be considered a slum in LA was affluence beyond the imagination here. The suburban house built of a deodorant ad, where Jennifer and Sam had spoken to him this morning, would be considered a palace. The disparity between rich and poor hadn't hit him so hard since his radical days, when he and Jesús and a group of troublemakers had smeared themselves with ketchup and carried *Eat the Rich* placards into some bank on Market Street. *Because it's never too late to make a first impression.*

His brother slept in the seat beside him. He'd taken to drinking beer again, ostensibly because the water was bad, and this made him much easier to be around. Angelo found him a kinder, gentler Paul after a few Negra Modelos. Also, he'd shaved his Santa Claus beard and accepted, along with the plane ticket, some new clothes.

Popocateptl loomed like a purple wave over the city of eternal spring as the bus descended a snaky highway in twilight. Angelo had read that Cuernavaca was a favorite for summer hideaways because of its lovely climate and proximity to the capital, that Cortez and Maximilian, even the shah of Iran, had kept secret palaces here. Weird to think that their step-uncle, the guy who'd inspired religion in Paulie and political vandalism in Penny, may have found refuge where, for centuries, despots and fat cats had hidden out.

That evening Angelo called his daughter, and Sam asked about volcanic eruptions. Mom says you're right under a huge volcano which could blow any day.

Jennifer's voice was sweet. All our daughter can do is talk about your adventure. She really wishes you'd taken her along.

His adventure. After he hung up he thought about the way she'd said that, the hint of, what, admiration? A memory of how Jenn used to speak when his life had seemed more interesting to her? He stood before the mirror, a middle-aged guy with extra pounds and a receding hairline, and thought about his adventure.

At five in the morning Angelo awoke and realized that his brother was missing. He waited for first light to go looking for him. Some of the streets he called his brother's name down were narrow and cobbled, others wide and filled with commercial logos. Everything was drenched and oozing with the morning's warmth. Bird-of-paradise along walls with glimmering glass set into their tops to slice the fingers of the poor. A church with a garden of exotic flowers and a few bats coming in from the night, like shattered pieces of the night sky gathering under the church eaves. The streets led him to the *mercado,* which was in a ravine with the volcano towering over its end, and among the vendors who were setting up stalls and stoves or simply laying out their blankets of limes and potatoes he found his brother.

Paulie sat with a beer and a Bible, leaning against a wall in the ravine. Angelo asked him where he'd spent the night.

The school wasn't open.

No kidding? Not at three in the morning? Angelo squatted beside him. The nerve of some people. His brother stared off somewhere, he guessed at the mountain. So, what do you think?

Paul was silent for a moment. Then he smiled. I love this place. I absolutely love this place.

They waited until eight to knock on the door of the school, which was really an old house with an enclosed patio. Paul started to speak Spanish, and Angelo listened and tried to understand. He saw his brother produce the wrinkled newspaper articles which he and Lorna Dee and Kathy Manslayer had been gathering from the Spanish-speaking press, *La Prensa de Milagros.* The blond woman, who spoke Spanish with a Scandinavian accent, seemed to know Señor Almas very well. Paul's voice was rich with excitement.

Angelo had to jog to keep up with him. They found Fernando Almas asleep under an old Chevy Nova. He crawled out to shake their hands. The articles he'd written, yes, Angelo understood a little of what they were saying about these reports of a miracle healer named Verbizcaro, almost the same last name as theirs. Jesús Gómez de Verbizcaro, and he didn't practice here but in the Yucatán, where the palm is.

Oh, great, Angelo said. He asked Paul to translate some questions for the reporter about this Jesús of the miraculous healing powers who supposedly lived under a weeping coconut palm which, when photographed from a certain angle, looked a lot like a profile of Mother Mary or, in Angelo's estimation, a praying mantis.

Cuantos años tiene Jesús?

The reporter raised his hands and guessed about twenty-five. The photo of the man beneath the miraculous palm tree looked like a twenty-five-year-old with long hair who could be the Jesús they sought if he'd never aged a day in the past thirty years.

Paulie, he would be fifty-five by now. Not like this guy in the picture.

He called Jennifer an hour later. We haven't spoken this much for months, he mused.

Right.

Listen, we have to go clear out to the Yucatán, and it looks like we're going by bus. I guess he's at some place in Quintana Roo.

Oh, my God, that is supposed to be paradise, Jennifer said. Oh, God, Sam will die of envy. I wish she could be there with you. You could go snorkeling.

Well, I couldn't fly her down there. I mean, she's way too young to fly alone.

All she talks about is you and Mexico.

Paulie is obsessed with finding this guy. I hope it doesn't break his heart because this sham of the weeping coconuts can't be our uncle. Anyway, my agent, and Paulie's desperation, twisted my arm.

Maybe I should bring her. I don't even have a good swimming suit.

Your blue one looks great.

Forty minutes before their bus took off he couldn't find his brother again. He ran through the afternoon downpour, the rainwater cascading down church steps, a plastic poncho flapping around him like wings, and felt more foolish than ever. Inviting Jennifer to meet him in the Caribbean paradise, losing track of his crazy brother, not even certain how or where to find the faith healer or sham shaman that almost undoubtedly wasn't the Jesús of their youth. He ran through the tropical deluge, flapping his yellow wings like Big Bird as cars and motor scooters roared past. He found Paul in the churchyard, which was called Jardin de Bodas, or wedding garden. He thought of his heart pounding under the poncho like a little pouch of blood, he thought of weddings and Jennifer and eternal spring, he thought of the word *sangre* as he told his brother they had to run for the Red Arrow or wait two days for the next chance.

Paul got up from the slab of marble he'd been kneeling on. His white hair and dirty white shirt and pants were soaked. Without a word, he ran.

He couldn't put her out of his mind for ten minutes. Would they share a bed? Would it even be safe, in every respect of that word, since she'd slept with Charles in the interim, and he had spent one night with a coworker named Denise? Whenever the bus stopped, blind men and musicians would board, begging for pesos, sometimes selling tamales, and Angelo thought of men who would maybe kill a person like Charles for sleeping with their wives. It was an old Bluebird bus, the kind he and his brother had ridden to school over forty years ago, and chickens and goats were occasional passengers. They made their way over mountain ranges with the windows rattling and the goats complaining, and Angelo imagined himself with a straw sombrero and a machete, coming up to Charles at his Laguna Beach office and shouting, in a thick Spanish accent, You touch my wife and I keel you! I keel you!

Angelo fell asleep thinking of his daughter and her mother. He awoke when the bus came to a stop. They were on the shoulder of a dark highway. He wondered if they were waiting to take on passengers, or if an accident or obstruction blocked their passage. The driver got up and spread a bedroll down the aisle between the seats, then lay on it. He heard some passengers sigh with a little exasperation in their throats. The driver started snoring. People got out to relieve themselves in the bushes, Paul among them. He never reboarded.

The bus started up an hour later. Angelo was calling in the

darkness near the highway for his brother. For Christ's sake, Paulie, don't do this! Paulie! The bus took off.

Some time later they were sitting in the dim light just before dawn, beside a road which stretched across miles of mountainous forest. Paul looked at Angelo and said, You know what you are? You're a doubting Thomas.

Really? Angelo tried to hide the anger in his voice. Imagine that. Doubt.

Don't take offense. Your skepticism and wit serve you really well, for the most part. But you won't believe until God shows his face to you, will you?

Well. Angelo rubbed his eyes. The light was softly giving the trees their colors. How does, or how will, God show his face to me?

Somebody we both knew, somebody who changed our lives, was filled with God's grace, and you can't accept that. But we are going to see him again.

I'll admit that he was charismatic and kind of, I don't know. He yawned. Kind of radiant. Is that good enough? But you don't know if this guy Verbizcaro is him or not, do you?

Paul stared at him for a while. Angelo could see the flecks of green in his brother's brown eyes. Paul smiled. He looked younger, almost as he had as a high school baseball star. You don't understand the spirit of Jesus.

Our Jesús, the kid I cleaned toilets with, was the actual guy from Nazareth, you're saying?

No. That's not what I'm saying.

And when that drunk guy shot him, he died for our sins, but you think he's really alive? The sky was turning from purple and black to a soft whitish-blue. An expensive-looking car approached, and Angelo tried to flag it down. Stop, you sons of bitches!

I think there's no such thing as death. Not really. There's really only love, and life.

And there's only about one car an hour on this fucking road, Paulie.

Paul. The rich people won't stop, but some poor man will come along, soon.

Not fifteen minutes later a beat-up pickup truck clanked up to them. Angelo and Paul climbed in back with a large pig. To the Ritz-Carlton, Jeeves, Angelo said to the pig. The truck bounced through the mountains to a village, where they spent much of the day arranging for further transportation, Paul doing the talking. Angelo guessed that all those years in the Southwest had at least given Paulie some grasp of a second language.

The next morning, somewhere on the Gulf coast, they stopped and had *huevos rancheros.* The bus would be delayed, a man at the counter said. Maybe two hours. Maybe more. Angelo would be at least one day, possibly two, late in meeting his daughter and wife, or estranged wife. He would try to leave a message at their hotel. They walked on the beach of this Gulf city, Coatzalcoalcos, which smelled of petroleum, and came back. Now the guy at the station said the bus would be ready that night or the next morning. Who knows? *Quien sabe?*

Angelo followed his brother, who seemed to need to keep moving, all around the town. He repeated the bus clerk's phrase over and over, *quien sabe, quien sabe,* trying to get that world-weary inflection perfectly. Sometimes Paul said he was listening to God speak to him and asked Angelo to be quiet. *Ay, dios,* Angelo said. *Quien sabe?*

They went to a five-year-old, dubbed George Clooney movie, and an explosion shook the seats in the middle of the film, and the theater went totally dark. They groped their way outside and saw that the entire city was blacked out. Paul laughed. When the lights came back on, the people walking the promenade near the beach cheered and clapped.

A bus came into town. Angelo and Paul happened to see it from the promenade. They ran for it and boarded just in time. It rolled along a fairly level terrain, and the sweet smells of the tropics washed across them from the loose windows. Angelo fell asleep, thinking of the perfume of trees and women, thinking of his daughter's hair after her evening bath. When he awoke his brother was standing outside, near his window, speaking to a man. Angelo wasn't sure if he was awake or still dreaming because the view of Paul through the smudged window seemed unreal at first. Paul looked as he had when he was a little boy. He and the man squatted and drew circles and lines in the dirt. The man's hair was black and shiny as a beetle. He and Paul stood and embraced.

This place is holy land, Paul told him. He listed some of the reasons: the Mayan pyramids, the sacrificial cenotes, the ancient ruins covered by jungle vines, the old Franciscan churches. We're very close, now, he said. Very close!

They ate bananas and avocados in the jungle city of Valladolid. Paul arranged for the bus to the shrine of the weeping palms, and Angelo paid, as always. He caught a reflection of himself in a shop window and was shocked to see this haggard, whiskered person staring back. It took hours to reach the shrine, and it looked to be a commercial success with its billboards and souvenir stands. Decals of the Virgin of Guadalupe, hand-carved crosses with bleeding Christs, and garish paintings and postcards of the weeping coconut palm spread before them on blankets where smooth-faced people hawked them. The palm itself was surrounded by tourists, most of them Mexicans, snapping pictures. It looked no different from any of the other trees, in Angelo's estimation, except that it leaned lower, as if a recent hurricane had almost uprooted it. He paid for their audience with the healer, and they stood in line.

Following the local custom, Paul dropped to the floor of the little wooden chapel and crawled the distance to his seat in a pew. Angelo didn't prostrate himself, but he crossed and genuflected. The healer spoke in a singsong Spanish, and people crawled up to him and offered their heads to his hands. He looked to be about thirty and well-fed. The puffiness around his eyes betrayed a habit of drinking. Angelo watched his brother receive the blessing of hands and crawl back to his pew. The smile on Paul's face was like Samantha's over a hot-fudge sundae.

Excuse me. Angelo had waded among the faithful to the pulpit. Many had left the chapel to make purchases, but he knew that Paul was still kneeling behind him among the most fervent visitors. He knelt before the stout man and studied his face. You're not the Jesús we knew, I mean the Jesús from our family. I'm Angelo Verbicaro, and that's my brother, Paul.

The healer raised his eyebrows. He placed his hands on Angelo's head.

Ouch, hey, you don't need to do that, Angelo said.

The man chanted something in Spanish. The only words Angelo understood were *muchos años,* or many years.

Some time later he waited for the bus to Cancún. He would see Jennifer and Samantha, and they might be a family again, or they might simply see how separate their lives must remain. Paul hugged him and sighed. His smile seemed unable to undo itself, and he kept saying, Wow.

I'm glad it was so good for you, Angelo said. Do you need a cigarette or something?

Did you feel it, Angie?

The sun was sinking into the trees.

I don't think so. Did I feel it? I guess not. Actually, I felt some pain. Anyway, I'm sorry.

Don't be sorry.

But we came all this way, and it wasn't him.

Paul touched his face and turned it to him, as a child might to make sure you're listening to everything he's saying. It *was* him, Angie. We recognized each other. He recognized you.

Angelo started to respond, then shrugged and remained silent. The Jesús he'd known was as American as himself, a Chicano kid raised in California and the racist Rocky Mountain states of the USA. He was probably three inches taller than the Mexican shaman or con man they'd met today, and if he hadn't been shot by a drunk in San Francisco he would be fifty years old by now, not thirty. Angelo saw no sense in mentioning any of this to his brother, however. Instead he asked Paul to tell him what the man had said while his hands were on his scalp.

He said that after many years, wait, how did he say it? Something like, after many years you once again see the face of the beloved.

ngelo sat alone in the dark as the bus flew under the black branches, as the frilly plastic tassels and religious icons swished across the windshield to protect the driver and his passengers while they roared through the jungle. The face of his wife, after a matter of weeks, of months since the separation: Wasn't this the face of his beloved? Perhaps it *had* been years since they had looked upon each other, had really looked into each other's faces, with love.

t required more hours of waiting to catch a ferry from Puerto Juárez to the island. The slow boat to Isla Mujeres reminded him of a Mississippi steamboat, its striped awning charred by the smoke of its engine. The water was the green-blue of Jennifer's eyes. He found them soon enough, and their beauty together, mother and daughter wading in the surf, made him feel weightless.

What's with your hair? Samantha asked.

My hair?

Yes, Jennifer asked, what *is* with your hair? It reminds me of those old-fashioned flattops with wings.

You have white wings, Dad.

I don't have enough hair for wings. What are you talking about?

So, how was Jesús?

Angelo sighed. His daughter had her arms wrapped around his neck, her hands probing the sides of his head. Well, he wasn't Jesús, but Paulie thinks he was, so I didn't want to burst his balloon.

You've got horns, too, Samantha said.

Hey! Angelo moved her hand and touched a bump on the side of his head. Feels like a big spider bite.

Where is your brother, Paulie?

He saw me off at the ferry. He got connected somehow with some guys on the mainland. He felt the other bump and laughed. Weird. Two bumps, like horns, all right. I don't know, Paulie's gone native or something, but he seemed more sane and relaxed than I've seen him in years. I think he's working with a bunch of farmers and devotees on some kind of export deal with his hippie commune.

You look happy about it, Jennifer said. The wind lifted her hair, moved it slowly across her shoulder.

I guess I am, Angelo said.

Your hair looks like fingers, Samantha said. Not wings.

That afternoon Sam and Jennifer went to the market and an Internet café while Angelo swam. He swam past the rope border, among fishing and tourist boats, farther than he felt was reasonable, then farther than he felt was safe. The current took him north. He went under now and then and came up. He studied the rolling line of blue across his eyes. That sense of two worlds, of light and dark, and how easy it would be to let go and give in. Exhausted, he lay back and rocked on the deep.

A black shape floated high above him. It looked like a cross, but in a while he saw that it was a bird, a pelican come to observe him there, a fish too big for its beak. He peered at the distant shore and thought about his daughter, and how horrible it would be for her if he didn't make it back. A boat full of scuba divers picked him up.

When he staggered onto the beach Jennifer was waiting for him with a towel. She told him that Sam was with a friend at the Internet café. They walked in their swimsuits through town to the little hotel room, his muscles feeling heavy from their work, and few words were exchanged before they made love on the bed in the leafy shadow of a bamboo and the racket of birds in the window. Afterward Angelo cried, and Jennifer stroked his head against her breast.

I'm so sorry, Angelo, she said, crying also. I'm so, so sorry. I made a horrible mistake.

What are we going to do?

Can we get back? I couldn't live without Sam this summer.

We both need Sam. Sam needs us.

Her hand lingered on his hair. What does this mean?

I have no idea. He wiped his eyes. What *does* it mean? Are we back, or what?

Lift your head a minute. She gazed at him with large, moist eyes. They *are* like fingers, Sam's right. Like white fingers painted onto your black hair.

He walked into the bathroom and saw a strange naked man with a stubbly, sunburned face framed by the white imprint of hands on the sides of his head, and he burst out laughing. I'll be damned, he said. I look like Hawk Boy.

Come back to bed, Hawk Boy.

He went to the market for mangos and pastries, noticing the looks he got from the local people. He heard some of them say *pelo,* and some *manos.* He had the imprint of the healer's hands on his hair, some trick the man had pulled on him, and it made him laugh aloud in public. He wondered how long it would last. He stood above the beach and watched the sun set over the fishing boats, trying to contain his laughter.

When he returned to the room, Jenn was asleep on the bed they'd made love in, and Samantha was reading a book about knights and ladies. She whispered to him that their friend Naomi wanted to see him at this bar on the beach in an hour.

What are you talking about, Monkey? he whispered back.

Mom and I have been getting to know your fairy godmother. Aunt Naomi's here, Samantha said to his look of confusion. She is so cool. She said your story was a big deal to her, or something. Also, she said she needed an excuse to lie in the sun.

I'll be damned. She's here in Isla Mujeres.

Why does she make you mad?

Am I mad? I don't know. Literary agents are hard to figure out.

Angelo held his daughter on the balcony and read to her, then put her to bed beside her mother. Jenn's hair fanned back, and moonlight dappled her cheek and shoulder. Sam said she'd rather go with him to see Aunt Naomi.

I'm afraid not. This is business I need to take care of.

Are you staying here tonight, Dad?

Yes.

Yay! She hugged his neck. You people are weird.

I know. He kissed the top of her head. But we love each other. No matter how weird, don't forget that we all love each other. We have a lot of work to do.

There goes your laptop.

I'm afraid my lapper's in California.

I hear it tinkling. No, it's something else. Listen. It's out there.

He knelt beside his daughter, in silence and deep happiness, and canted his head to one side, imitating her gesture. There was distant motor-scooter traffic, some kind of cricket or cicada, and something else. What is that? he whispered.

Shh. Sounds kind of like singing, and kind of like glass, she said. Like glass rubbing against the sky. Maybe it's the moon.

A glass moon. *Quien sabe?*

He walked to the café, thinking of beauty and loss and the music of the moon, the music of the spheres. He thought of his wife and daughter, of their hearts being little *bolsas,* purses of beauty, filled with a kind of celestial light which he could never possess, but never entirely lose, either.

A lightning storm flashed and rumbled in the direction of the Cancún hotel skyline, and as it had in the town of Coatzalcoalcos, the electric power of Isla Mujeres snuffed after an explosive sound from somewhere south of town. A few people sighed or laughed, and a few candles were lit. He fumbled along La Avenida Hidalgo to the café and sat in darkness at a table overlooking the sea. These people are so accustomed to losing power, he thought.

He saw the figure of a woman approach.

That you, Angelo?

It isn't Lazarus risen from the dead, he replied. Or even Lazaro Cara, for that matter, he said to himself. They hugged in the dark, then sat across the table from each other. His heart beat rapidly, and sweat dripped down his shirt. He could barely see her silhouette against the dim expanse of the sea.

Samantha is an absolute angel. So, where's Paulie?

Angelo told her about Paul's decision to stay on the peninsula a while to make a deal with a coffee co-op, and he briefly described their differing experiences at the shrine of the weeping palm.

So, Naomi said, you have a split decision on Jesús. One is based on cool logic, the other on passionate faith.

Why do I feel like you're putting me down when you say that?

I'm not putting you down.

Never mind. So, tell me the story of Naomi Ginsburg-Menendez. Where does this odd ethnic mix come from?

She coughed. Naomi Ginsburg was born and raised in Pittsburgh, she said, speaking of herself in the third person, went to Carnegie Mellon to study art history, and flew to Mexico in the early '70s seeking an experimental cure for terminal cancer. There she met a bunch of other expatriates and ne'er-do-wells from the States, political radicals and drug smugglers, fugitives, idealists, and dreamers. That was in San Miguel de Allende.

San Miguel de Allende, the little pueblo south of the border where you started *la vida nueva*.

Yes, I started a new life, Angelo. I married a Cuban Marxist and took on a new name. We moved to New York in the early '80s, and I've been there ever since, first working in publications, then as a literary agent for a wonderful, understanding woman.

She must have been a very understanding woman when you made five or six bucks selling my story about Pelican Island to a magazine with thirty readers. That took some big balls.

Why are you . . . ? Her voice trailed off. They sat a moment in silence. Do you have any idea why I'm here?

I have been asking myself the same thing. Actually, I've been asking myself why I am here with you and my daughter and my estranged wife, in a place called "the island of women."

Estranged? Her hand touched his wrist.

I don't know. *Quien sabe?* He could hear distant thunder and a few women's voices making bird-like exclamations. He thought of the feeling of Jenn's hands on his shoulders that afternoon, and his daughter's skinny arms around his neck, and now the pressure of this dry, small hand squeezing his in the dark. No, not estranged, he said. We're going to make a go of it again.

Good, good.

But I ask myself all the time lately how it is we got where we are. Why did some little girl write a ransom note in Italy and have to run away to America, for instance?

Children are innocent, she said. Children deserve forgiveness.

It's an old story, and my bet is she did it for love, Angelo said. There was a handsome crook she wanted to impress.

Is love why people do terrible things? She made a sound: a laugh, a cry? He couldn't tell. Look, I have two kids who are grown now, a grandchild, and a husband who is supportive of almost everything except the decision I've recently made to make amends for something I did in my youth.

He squeezed her hand as if one or the other of them were about to slip over the edge of a cliff. Amends? he whispered. Amends?

I believed in something so strongly, she said in hushed tones, and hated our government so much for what it had done to my brother and to a young man and his cause, that I helped the man I was living with commit a serious crime.

Angelo felt light-headed. He felt as if the wing-like hairs on his head beat quietly and lifted him from the table. The tiny lights of two candles were moving toward him, a young man's face floating dimly above their flames. He could remember the sensation of the shaman's hands on his scalp. Somewhere in the faraway darkness of the beach women were singing in high, dolorous tones, keening in a language he couldn't understand.

The night janitor, a retarded boy, so much like my sister, always left work before midnight, and we knew this, but that one night I guess he fell asleep in the office. Her voice caught before she went on: We burned him, along with the names and files in the draft board. We set fire to a building and killed this innocent boy, and I've struggled not to hate myself just long enough to raise my children. Now I'd like it if you and Paulie would help me turn myself in.

Whatever you need, he said helplessly, knowing that she was always the older and wiser one, he the eternal dumb kid.

The candles alighted on their table like small birds. In their glow Angelo saw her face, an old woman's small face now, but familiar beyond the passage of years and beautiful beyond imagining. He took his glasses off and wiped his eyes. Whatever you need, we'll work together.

ACKNOWLEDGMENTS

First, I want to thank my wife, Ellen and my daughter, Emily. They not only believed in my writing, they gave me the time and place to do it. Without their loving encouragement this book wouldn't have been written.

Second, I owe so much to Greg Michalson for his stewardship in the creation of this book. I can't say enough about his editorial insights. All of us who struggle with the muse are lucky to have him in this business.

I'd like to thank the editors at a few literary magazines for working with me and finding a place in their journals for some of the stories this book began with: Peter Stine, Kenneth Pellow, Gina Frangello and Theresa Berger. I'd also like to thank Oregon Literary Arts for an award early in the writing.

Some fine writers who happen to be dear friends have encouraged me as I worked on this manuscript, particularly Rick Borsten, John Witte, Deb Casey, and Bruce Campbell.

Most importantly, I can't begin to thank my family enough for their tolerance and support, especially my wise and courageous father, Frank, my loving and talented mother, Sheila, my brilliant sister, Linda, and my hilarious brother, Frank. My lovely aunts, uncles and cousins, most of whom have passed on, are too numerous to list here. A more delightful and generous group of people is hard to find.

Finally, I would like to dedicate this book to my grandparents, Luisa and Vito Addiego, and raise a salute to Vito's birthplace in Calabria, a hillside village called Verbicaro.